Other Works by Cort Fernald

Algonquin

Sisters' Secret

Keeper of an Ordinary

Keeper Trial and Vengeance

West of Antipathy

KEEPER

COUP DE GRACE

CORT FERNALD

Publisher's Note: *Keeper Coup de Grace* is a work of fiction. Names, characters, places, and incidents are a product of the author's imagination. Locales and public names are sometimes used for atmospheric purposes. Any resemblance to actual people, living or dead, or businesses, companies, events, institutions, or locales is entirely coincidental.

Keeper Coup de Grace / Cort Fernald. – 1st edition
ISBN-978-0-578-68173-3

ACKNOWLEDGMENTS

My heartfelt thanks to my editor Sue Michels for the invaluable advice, support and assistance with editing, formatting text and creating the cover for all of my published books. She has been instrumental in my career as a writer for the past 13 years.

Also, many thanks to my brother-in-law and best friend Tony Williams and my sister Rusty Hendley, for their unwavering support and critique throughout my writing career.

And my thanks to the Nebraska Thriller Group, Victoria G and Terry N for their thoughtful and helpful critique on *Keeper Coup de Grace.*

INTRODUCTION

Keeper Coup de Grace is the third novel in the *Keeper* series. It is hoped these contemporary thrillers have been as enjoyable for readers as it has been for me to write them.

Keeper of an Ordinary was the first in the series and set the tone of an everyman caught up in a nightmare of violence with the Russian Mafia.

Rich Rice is a journalist at a south suburban Chicago newspaper. He might still be at that newspaper had his publisher not come into possession of a notebook outlining the human trafficking and prostitution activities of a Russian Mafia family—the Franko's. Rich is given the assignment and his articles earn him the ire of the Russians.

After an assassination attempt, Rich goes on the lam. He leaves his wife Gisele at her mother's in Glencoe thinking she would be safe. Rich heads west—landing in Omaha. To survive he buys and opens a small bar in South Omaha naming it The Ordinary.

Suka Franko, the Russian Mafia madam of the Franko family is the daughter of ex-KGB general Ivan Franko. She, and her gun-crazy son Nickolai, go after Rich and via a ruse, find him. A terrific gunfight at The Ordinary ensues. Rich manages to kill Nicky.

Rich learns Suka has abducted Gisele and Rich races to Glencoe. In the gunfight, Rich manages to wound Suka and free Gisele. But Suka gets away on a speedboat.

Keeper Trial & Vengeance picks up with Suka's escape and rendezvous with a Russian freighter in the Great Lakes.

Rich is tried before a Grand Jury and investigated for possible indictment of murder with the death of Nicky at The Ordinary shoot-out. While the Grand Jury deliberates Rich meets with the FBI in Chicago.

The Grand Jury verdict comes in with a No Bill--Rich is not indicted. But Gisele has gone missing. Three days later her body is found in Omaha's notorious Hummel Park. Through informants, Rich finds out Suka is responsible for Gisele's death. She is hiding out in an abandoned KGB Villa in the Hill Station area of Northern India.

Rich vows vengeance and travels halfway around the world to India. There he confronts Suka and Russian Mafia members of the gang.

Keeper Coup de Grace follows Rich's return to the United States. Grieving for his wife Gisele, Rich wants only to be left alone. But through an Omaha Police CCTV video Rich learns his vengeance is not yet fulfilled.

CHAPTER 1

The smell of hamburgers frying on a griddle drifted up the dark street, carried on the bone-chilling wind. Smoke and odor curled out the galvanized stovepipe atop The Ordinary bar on the corner of 16th street and Vinton. A crack of narrow white light leaked out the propped-open back door and pie-sliced across the gravel lot.

Rich Rice limped toward the rear of The Ordinary, pausing only to let the pain from his wounded left foot subside. He adjusted the shoulder strap of his pack, clutched the handle of his laptop case, and set off again.

B-b-b-back in the USA, he thought.

He trembled, with only a t-shirt and hooded sweatshirt, a barrier between himself and the bite of early winter air.

Rich glanced over his shoulder at the red taillights on the back of the black SUV disappearing up 16th

Street. The Assistant to Deputy Director Southeast Asia Honesto Ogg, and a pair of suits had dropped Rich off.

"Hope I never see you again," Rich had told him as he gingerly stepped out of the SUV. An electric shock ran up his leg when he put weight on his left foot.

"Don't be so sure of that," the short man laughed, huddled in his trench coat in the back seat. "We'll take you to a doc."

"No way. Go fuck yourself." Rich slammed the heavy door.

"Fuck you too," came the muffled reply before the SUV roared off.

Slowly, painfully, with halting steps, he made his way across the gravel lot. Small berms of black-capped snow, old snow, rung the lot. His white F-150 was parked by the green and rust-colored dumpster, where he had left it. There was no snow on the hood and roof, and tire tracks in and out. Someone had driven it since the snow.

There was an empty spot next to his truck where Gisele's Honda should've been parked. In the police impound yard, covered by a blue tarp, Rich figured. He couldn't stop the memories of seeing her car abandoned in Hummel Park and the shotgun blast hole on the passenger side windshield.

He missed her every moment of every day.

He unshouldered his pack and let it drop next to the rear door. He lay the laptop next to it. His back to the cold brick, he eased himself down. The pain in his foot had become a throbbing ache. Tolerable, barely. Maybe the stitches had pulled loose. That Indian pharmacist was no doctor. He'd tied him up as best he could. They both knew Rich couldn't go to the hospital with a gunshot wound.

A bouncy concertina, Mexican music, could be heard from inside. The aroma of hamburgers grew stronger.

Rich's stomach made a growling noise. He tried to recall his last meal. Rice and chicken, at the West View Inn in Ranikhet, the Hill Station area of Northern India. Maybe two days ago? He didn't eat when he got back to Delhi. He didn't eat in Odessa. He didn't eat changing planes in Frankfurt, nor arriving at O'Hare. And when Agent Ogg snagged him at O'Hare and flew him back to Omaha on a CIA twin-engine executive jet, there was no food offered.

He had no idea what day it was—weekday or weekend. The days had no name. Forty-eight hours before, he had exacted vengeance, killing those responsible for killing his wife Gisele.

The knot in his chest twisted the anger in his soul. The faces of those he'd killed swam across his thoughts. He had no satisfaction in his heart.

The wind kicked up. Rich hugged his knees for warmth.

Gisele.

Blood on his hands. The angry world at his back. The smell of grilling beef up his nose. He'd been changed and barely recognized himself. He missed Gisele terribly. She could always bring him up when he was down; take him out of himself when he became too self-absorbed; and say one word when he was going down the wrong path. Would she love him now—after all he'd done to those that murdered her?

No. She would not.

He struggled upright, grappling up the wall. Most of his weight he kept on his right foot. Rich looped his arm through the pack.

The light almost blinded him as he slowly pulled open the back door. Music, a wave of warm air and a strong smell of cooking overwhelmed him.

Jorge, wearing a grease-stained white apron over black Levi's and a plain white tee, with a hairnet crowning his narrow acne-scarred face, stood at the griddle, jiggling and tapping the spatula in time to the music.

The door banged. Jorge wheeled, a filet knife grabbed from a magnetic holder on the wall held low and ready.

"*No pieces entrar aquí, Cabron,*" he snarled.

Seeing the long thin blade, Rich slid his right foot back and brought his hands up and open. He waited for the thrust and readied himself to fend off the knife hand, roll, then grab the wrist, bringing his left palm up and through the elbow.

Jorge's expression changed; his angry face now questioned. "*Jefe?*"

"Jorge," Rich croaked, snapping out of it. He took a deep breath and coughed. "*Tranquillo.*"

The Hispanic cook approached, squinting, standing before Rich. "It not you. You...all right?"

"Yeah." Rich cleared his throat. "I'm okay."

"Ay...You look sick."

"Sick?" Rich glimpsed his face in the blurry reflection on the stainless-steel refrigerator, His face with dark, sunken eyes stared back. "I could use a burger."

"What on your sleeve, *Jefe?*"

Rich glanced down. The blood had dried long ago and turned to deep maroon stains. "Nothing."

"I finish order and make you burger."

"Thanks. Who's on the floor?"

Jorge put the knife back on the wall. "*Es* busy night. Everybody here."

Rich cautiously pushed open the kitchen door. The bar was lit by neon and small multicolored lights on the walls, with candles lighting the tables and booths. Shadowy shapes filled the bar. A good crowd.

Someone stood at a microphone on the stage to the right of the kitchen door, emphatically enunciating:

"Men are winning...

Hypocrites are leading

The sheep follow...

to the shearing..."

Rich stepped back and let the kitchen door close.

"What is this, Jorge?"

Jorge shrugged, flipping a burger. "Is poetry. Daisy thing. All I know is burger, burger, *mucho* burger."

Rich took a step on his wounded foot and grimaced.

"You hurt, *Jefe?*"

"I'm all right."

He slipped out of the kitchen and into the barroom. Tables were full. The long bar had only a few vacant stools. Daisy, with a big smile, carried a round tray of six beers, and two stem glasses of wine, weaving through tables to a booth at the end.

On stage, a large bearded man in flannel shirt and jeans, lit by a small spotlight that made his forehead and bald spot shine, read from an open book, emphasizing each word with his free hand.

At the center of the bar, Riku was stooped over making drinks. Flanking him were two shapely statuesque Japanese girls with pale complexions, large dark eyes, long black hair and wearing matching red silk embroidered dresses. Young men crowded two-deep at the bar in front of the girls. They were clearing the bar of empties, wiping the top, and placing full beers before patrons.

Limping, Rich made his way to the POS station at the bar end.

Riku was the first to recognize him.

"Keeper." His round face broke into a smile and he slipped behind one of the Japanese girls. "You're back."

Rich settled onto a stool. "Riku," he was breathless. "It is good to see you. Yes, I'm back."

They shook hands. "Happy you're back."

Rich pointed to the two girls. "Your sisters?"

"Yes. And look at all the guys." Riku pointed to the girl at the front of the bar. "That's Ami." Then he motioned to the girl behind him. "And this is Yumi."

She turned, confused her name had been called. She smiled at Rich.

Riku moved closer, giving Rich a searching look. "Are you okay?"

"Fine."

"You're looking, ah, tired."

"Well, yeah, just a little."

Daisy paused at a table, bending to talk.

The poet droned on:

"Women kill...

With kindness.

They steal...

With a smile.

They seduce...

With a promise.

They leave...

At midnight.

Sneaking back to their husbands and sweethearts."

Rich watched Daisy. She commanded the floor. Slender and tall, with a childlike face and high cheekbones surrounded by a stylishly wild natural. Her big, warm smile of good white teeth and the twinkle in her eyes, reiterated her youth and vibrance. Rich knew deep down, she grieved as he. Maybe six weeks or a month ago that Tom Waller, her perfect match, was gunned down, right there behind the bar. Daisy maneuvered through tables, deftly placing full glasses around while plucking empties. To the kitchen and back to a booth, she set plates of hamburgers before a couple. Then she paused, making sure they had everything they needed.

He missed Gisele.

"Boss." Daisy all but ran the last few steps when she saw him at the bar. She stopped short, abruptly and self-conscious.

"Daisy," he wearily replied, leaning back.

"I'm, I'm happy you're back." Her eyes searched his face. "Are you okay?"

"Why is everybody asking me that. I'm fine. Just tired."

Ami yelled out for Riku, and he went up the bar.

Daisy stepped closer, deep concern in her eyes. She touched Rich's arm. "Sorry I asked. I've, ah, we've been worried about you."

"I got off a flight from..." Rich stopped.

Applause filled the bar for the poet.

"From where?" Daisy asked in his ear.

He could smell her perfume, sweet, fresh like cut flowers. "Never mind."

An overweight woman, in gray cable knit sweater, jeans and tennis shoes stepped up to the microphone. She pulled down the back of her sweater. "That con- cludes the poetry slam for tonight. I want to thank Daisy Wilson, manager of The Ordinary..."

Rich gave her a sidelong glance and a half smile. She averted her eyes. "Manager?" he whispered.

"...and all of you for coming out on this cold Thurs- day."

It's Thursday, Rich thought.

"...on behalf of the Omaha Poets Union. Look for us at other events and we will be here at The Ordinary, next month."

More applause, with people standing, sent her off the stage.

"Are you hungry?" Daisy asked.

"Jorge is making me a burger."

Daisy stared at him in silence. Rich met her gaze. He knew she had questions, but he wouldn't answer.

"Oh, Miss," someone at a table called out.

Daisy went to them.

Riku was at Rich's elbow. "What can I get you to drink?"

"Got any of the Rouge Ale left?"

"Cold Brewed IPA or Dead Guy Ale?"

"Dead Guy--that suits me."

The throbbing pain in his foot was getting more than he could bear. He pulled out loose change from his pocket and spilled it on the bar, hoping he still had a Vicodin. He poked through and found a caplet, blowing the lint off it.

Riku put a twelve-ounce glass of golden ale before Rich and picked up a coin. "Where's this from?"

Rich squinted, tossing the Vicodin in his mouth and taking a quick swallow. "That's twenty rupees."

"Rupees, like Indian rupees?" Riku picked up another coin. "And this one?"

"That's ten kopiyok." Rich took a longer drink to get the pill down his dry throat.

"Kopiyok? And that one looks like a Euro. Where you been, Keeper?"

"Not tonight, Riku." He pushed the coins into his palm and pocketed them.

The low rumble of conversation, sprinkled with laughter, filled the bar. Rich hated it.

"I want to play some music," he said to Riku.

"No," Daisy came up, blocking his hand. "Let me pick."

"Whose bar is it anyway?"

"It's yours, Boss. But I'm afraid of what you might pick." She poked numbers on the computer touch screen. "In your mood, you'd empty this place in a minute."

Pearl Jam's *Alive* came out of the barroom speakers. Rich listened and soundlessly seemed to laugh. "You forget I'm from the Northwest. I know what this song is about. You just read the title."

"I keyed in some Nirvana." She defended herself.

A bell rang in the kitchen.

"Oh," Rich replied sarcastically. "That's better?"

With a tight mouth, blazing eyes and nostrils flaring, Daisy stalked off to the kitchen. She was quickly back and banged the plate of hamburger and French fries a little too hard on the bar. The brown bun bounced off. Rich caught it. He looked at her and could tell he had hurt her.

"Daisy, I'm sorry. I haven't slept in probably forty-eight hours."

"Where were you?"

"It's none of your goddamn business."

He hurt her all over again and she darted out to the floor, picking up glasses and wiping tables.

The burger revolted him. It's not that he wasn't hungry, he was. But the idea of eating it sickened him. He picked it up in both hands and smelled the cooked meat. Just a small bite was all he could manage.

"My burger *es malo*?" Jorge asked.

"Your burger *mucho gusto*. I'm just too tired to eat."

"Lots of *Policia* come look for you while you gone."

"Who?" Rich wanted to know.

"*Dos* detectives."

"The two that told me about Gisele?"

"*Si*. And the tall *Federale*."

"Bertoloni, the FBI agent." Rich sipped his ale thoughtfully. "He's a long way from his office in Chicago. What did the detectives want?"

"Ay, Riku, *campanero*," Jorge called out, pointing. "Get that paper the *Policia* write for *Jefe*."

"Oh, yeah." Riku reached under the bar by the cash register and pulled out a folded note. He handed it to Rich.

His eyes could not focus on the writing. The bar was too dark. "I'll read it later." He refolded and pocketed the note.

"Your lawman, *el Gordo*, he come." Jorge lounged against the bar. "He say he know you gone but tell us call him if we hear from you."

"Did you feed him?" Rich managed a smile.

"Ay, I no feed him. He eat like *mi suegra*."

"You could've fed him."

"Ay, then *si*, I feed him burrito. But *uno*, just *uno* burrito." Jorge pushed off the bar. "I close kitchen." His face turned serious and he said in a low voice, "*Jefe, mi muy feliz* you back."

"Me too, *mi amigo*. Any foreigners come looking for me?"

"Foreigners?"

"Accents...men with accents."

"*Si*," Jorge's expression clouded over. "*Mucho malo tipo*."

"Tipo?"

"Dude."

"When?"

"When you go."

"What'd he look like?"

"*Ojos Muertos.*"

Rich looked, watched, and studied the silhouettes moving about the barroom. His nerves irritated him. An underlying rage made the walls too close, the darkness oppressive. He realized had Jorge not recognized him in the kitchen he would have killed the man. He had gone blood-simple and it worried him.

Daisy returned to the bar with a trayful of glasses. Her expression was set, and she purposely ignored Rich.

He leaned forward and poked her on the upper arm. "Daisy?"

She acted like she hadn't heard him.

"Daisy? Come on. Do you have my keys to the upstairs apartment?"

She pulled the keys out of her front pocket and clanged them on the bar.

Rich reached for the keys. Daisy took a sudden breath. He looked over at her. Her expression had changed. She appeared frightened. "What's the matter?"

"Boss, I have to tell you. I've, ah, I've been staying upstairs for the last couple of days."

'Yeah? So?" He didn't get what she was telling him.

"It was easy when I had early classes and we had a late night at the bar. I'll get my stuff out tomorrow."

It started to sink into Rich's weary brain, and it did not sit well with him. "You don't have any place to stay tonight?"

"No. I gave up my apartment and was staying with Mom." She looked as if she might start to cry. "She's not there tonight."

He exhaled through his nose a little too quickly, a little too sharp. "Okay. Okay. Don't wake me when you come up. Get your stuff out tomorrow." He saw she was relieved. He wasn't though. "It's fine, Daisy. Not a problem."

Rich slung his pack and picked up his laptop. "I'll see you tomorrow." He nodded and limped across the barroom, through the kitchen and out into the night. The ale had made him woozy and the pain in his foot seemed distant under the effects of the Vicodin. He took the long flight up the steel stairs one at a time to his apartment.

A gray layer of dust coated much of the kitchen counter and stovetop. There were Styrofoam food containers and cardboard pizza boxes strewn about the counter. A heavier layer of silence enveloped the apartment. An old, vaguely spoiled smell emanated from the dishes in the kitchen sink.

Still, cold air hung over the living room. Ambient orange light lit the apartment from street-side windows. But for the muffled music from the bar below, the apartment was deathly quiet. Rich felt along the wall by the door jamb, finding the switch. A ceiling light over the round table flashed on, as did a small lamp on an end table by the couch on the opposite wall.

He pushed back a pile of bar receipts, mail, circulars and FedEx packages, and placed his laptop on the table. One FedEx package had the return address of the FBI office; Roosevelt Road, Chicago. He flipped the package back on the pile. "Can't deal with that now."

He struggled to get the sweatshirt off his back and over his head, then draped it on the chair back.

The white towel that Gisele last used still hung on the handlebars of her stationary bike in the corner with the exercise equipment. He checked the thermostat—fifty-five degrees. He keyed in sixty-eight degrees. From the bowels of the building, he heard the fan kick in, humming air through the ventilators.

He stood at the bedroom door, reluctant to enter. Women's clothing was strewn about the room. The bedclothes were rumpled, unmade. Anger boiled up inside of him. He fought it, turning away.

Dirty jeans and shirts, odd bits of tickets and notes written in Hindi and Ukrainian, boarding passes for flights to Delhi, Odessa, Frankfurt, used Visa cards, a notebook and his passport, he took out of his day pack and heaped on the coffee table. With a small penknife, he cut the threads along the bottom seam of the pack. Out fell four gold Krugerrands he had carried just in case. From a side pocket, he fished out the taser flashlight and reserve power stick, universal electric plug, and Chinese knockoff mobile phone. Rich tapped the screen. "I'll be damned." He had two missed calls from numbers he did not recognize. He wondered if it was Vicky, his driver.

He hobbled a step at a time to the gun safe. He stood a moment at the door, his forehead to the cold metal while he tried to remember the combination. The black tumbler twirled and with a heavy click, Rich turned down the handle and opened the safe. He dropped the Krugerrands on a shelf and picked up his old burner phone. It still had some juice. Numbers scrolled from missed calls. Most were 847 area code. Rich recognized they were Gisele's mother in Glencoe, Illinois. Too late to call. He traded the phone for his dad's Colt Government M1911 automatic. Heavy in his hand, the weight of the wood and iron reassured him. He pulled back the receiver and checked the action, then smacked in a new magazine and let the receiver chamber a round.

In the bathroom were open zippered plastic pouches with makeup, brushes and other girl stuff. They had flowers all over them and had to be Daisy's. Rich looked away, stuffing down his anger all over again.

Too tired to shower, he got a couple of blankets from a closet and spread them on the couch.

Slowly, carefully, he unlaced and eased off his hiking boot. Sharp pain, like stepping on broken glass, went up his leg with every movement of his left foot. Without the numbing effect of the Vicodin, he would be screaming. Blood had seeped through his sock, drying brown and crisp. Grimacing he rolled down the sock. The bandage was dirty with old blood. It smelled. He sat slumped forward. He'd have to see a doctor tomorrow. All he could hope was the wound wasn't infected. After three days, his clothes peeled off his body like a snake's second skin. Balancing on the toe of his left foot, he went into the kitchen and turned on the stove light for Daisy, switching off the living room light.

Slipping between the blankets, he melted into the shadowy amber and quiet. He didn't believe he was there. Halfway around the world, he'd gone to exact vengeance for Gisele and kill the people that had killed her. He didn't think he'd return. Seeing Gisele's image behind his closed eyes, he wished he'd died there.

A sound like a shotgun blast startled Rich awake. For an instant, he thought himself lying in a pool of blood on the floor of General Ivan Franko's dacha in the Ukraine. His belly was shot away, his guts spread out across the floor. Dead eyes without a face, stared over him. Frantically he felt through the wet, sticky viscera for his automatic.

Where was he?

He shook, freezing and drenched in sweat.

A thin shadow drifted across the living room to the bedroom. A woman whispered, "Sorry."

CHAPTER 2

Hot coffee.

A shave. A shower, with his bandaged foot wrapped in a white plastic food storage bag.

He watched dawn inch over the Metro.

It all seemed familiar, yet not. Something was missing. He lived: his wife did not.

At the living room table, his laptop open, Rich lost himself updating bar receipts in his accounting app. Ten days of life as usual, though not his. Fragments of pulling a cold draft from the tap and placing it on the bar before a thirsty patron, mixed with grunts and struggling with the big Russian, until Rich found the knife on the ground and plunged it just below the Russian's sternum. He pushed the blade upward and deep until the gushing blood warmed his hand and wrist.

The receipts indicated no dip in the nightly take. But one evening, the money coming in spiked, nearly doubling. Rich checked the statements against bar tabs, receipts and everything matched. He made a mental note to ask Daisy about it. She had done well, even noting the amount she paid Riku's sisters from the till. She kept good books and Rich added to his note to compliment her and bump her salary.

He heard shots. He ducked. Then realized it was noise from the street outside.

Rich picked up the burner phone. Early, but not too early to call Gisele's mother. The line rang once, twice, then Frau Esslin answered in a frail, tentative voice.

"*Ja? Wer ist es*?"

"*Est* Richard."

"Richard? Richard," the older woman all but yelled. "*Wo bist du gewesen?*"

"*Mutter*, English. I've been..." he paused. "Away."

"I was worried about you."

"Thank you, *Mutter*."

"They take *mein* Gisele. I do not wish them to take you."

"They didn't."

"So much is going on. I don't know what to do. Richard...Gisele is being sued."

"Sued? I don't understand."

"One of her clients. She's being sued because... because she died?"

"Sounds like one of those rich bastards. They can't sue her, she, she's dead, but they can sue her estate."

"There are other things, Richard. Things she kept from you. She had a will."

"A will?"

"*Ja*, and she supported her brother Rudi."

"Ohhhhhh. No wonder he was so angry at me at Gisele's funeral. There went his meal ticket."

"Richard, that is cruel," his mother-in law-said. "It is so much *schlechte dinge.*"

Gisele would have called it *alles beschissen.*

"*Mutter*, how are you?" Rich asked.

"I have good days. I have bad days."

"I will come and see you very soon. I will take care of this lawsuit and the will," he reassured her. "If you need anything, call. Love you, *Mutter.*"

She was crying. "*Ja, Ich liebe dich.*"

Rich sorted through the pile of mail. The FedEx from FBI Agent Bertoloni was a meaningless letter about assisting Omaha Police investigating his wife's murder. The majority were bills, and insurance and funeral home sales pitches.

"Mornin'." Daisy stood in the bedroom door.

Rich glanced up, then quickly away. "Morning," he grumbled.

She wore no makeup on her sleepy face, bed wrecked hair, and a white t-shirt just long enough, but not long enough to cover her sleek bare legs. The neck hole had slipped off her shoulder.

"Is there coffee?"

"Mmm."

She padded barefoot across the living room.

He would not take his eyes off the computer screen. Anger started in the pit of his stomach. He focused on the accounting numbers to distract himself.

A mug of coffee held in both hands, on the couch, Daisy sipped. "Why's your foot bandaged?"

Rich clicked on another page and did not look over. "Stepped on a tack."

"You're not going to say what happened?"

"You don't need to be involved."

"Did Riku or Jorge tell you the people that came looking for you?" She took a long drink of coffee.

"Yeah." Reminded of the note from Omaha P.D., he asked, "Throw me my sweatshirt."

Daisy made a sour face, pinching Rich's hooded sweatshirt with thumb and forefinger. "Awww, this reeks." She carried it over.

Rich pulled out the note. A business card for Detective Sargent Forester was clipped to a note written with a ballpoint pen running out of ink. The combination of cursive and print stuttered all over the page. He asked Rich to call him. They had gathered evidence on suspects who may be involved in the murder of Gisele Rice. There was a number.

Rich tapped in the number on the phone dial pad. He'd meet and see their evidence, but he would never tell them that just days before he'd killed the men responsible for the murder of his wife.

"You've reached Detective John Forester. I am not at my desk. Please leave a detailed message and call back number. If this is a real emergency dial 9-1-1."

The line beeped.

"Detective Forester, this is Richard Rice..." He left his number and hung up.

Daisy bounced up. "Ahhh," she all but screamed. "I have class this morning. I'm going to jump into the shower. I'll pack up my stuff. Can you drive me to my grandmother's?" She scampered into the bathroom.

"Yeah," Rich said.

Daisy stepped backward down the iron steps in front of Rich as he slowly went one step down, one step down. She seemed to think she could catch him if he stumbled and fell. Rich recognized the oversized winter coat she wore.

"I'm all right, dammit."

The driver's seat to his pickup was way too forward and he had to slide it back to get in. Daisy climbed in with a green garbage bag full of her clothes and other stuff.

"Gran lives on 42nd off Ames, near Fontenelle Park." She clicked the seat belt. "Take the freeway to 480, then 75th to Ames."

Rich let the truck warm up. "Thanks for taking care of The Ordinary while I was gone. You did a great job."

Daisy gave a smug smile. "Didn't do much but get everyone in on time."

"I know it's a lot more than that. But thanks." Rich clicked on the window defroster. "I did have a question. There's one night, a Tuesday, when bar receipts doubled. How did that happen?"

"Oh, God...I know. That was the Japanese School Girl night. It was crazy."

"The what?"

"Japanese School Girl night."

"I don't understand."

"You did notice last night that Riku's twin sisters were dressed alike."

"Yeah."

"And that there were guys clustered at the bar at their station."

"Yeah."

"The twins like to dress up. They call it cosplay or something."

Rich put the truck in reverse and backed out of the parking spot.

"Mostly," Daisy said. "They dress nice. But that Tuesday they came in dressed in short, and I mean short, pleated plaid skirts, white knee socks, white blouses you could almost see-through and blue button-up sweaters."

"What?"

"And panties. White panties you could see. They had their hair in pigtails and all this makeup."

Rich checked left, then pulled out of the lot onto 16th Street, heading north.

"These guys started showing up. The ones there would text their pals they had to come and see the twins." Daisy's voice betrayed disgust. "They would drop dollar bills behind the bar so Yumi or Amy would have to bend over and pick them up."

"We're not having that happen again."

"Thank you. I told Riku. He just laughed." Daisy checked her phone. "I can talk to them."

"No, I'll talk to them. That's not the type of bar we're running."

They merged onto the freeway and drove toward the 480 Split.

"I need to know a good emergency room," Rich asked, scanning his mirrors and changing lanes to the left.

"There's 'Beggin' for Mercy'."

"What's that?"

"Bergin Mercy. It's over on 72nd and Mercy Street." She thought a second. "You probably wouldn't want to go to Emmanuel."

"Why?"

"Lots of gang-bangers. I've always heard that Methodist Hospital has a really good emergency. You should go there."

"The freeways in this town are poorly marked and goofy as hell. Where's Methodist Hospital?"

"On Dodge Street, at 84th street, I think." Daisy pointed ahead. "Get over or this lane will take you to Iowa."

They turned onto Ames and Rich recalled that he had looked at purchasing a bar nearby before he bought The Ordinary. The real estate agent had made a nasty comment, called the area "Dark Omaha." At a stoplight, a crowd of black kids crossing to Omaha North High School stared at them.

"What's that all about?"

"White man with a black girl." Daisy said it so matter-of-factly it startled Rich.

"So they think..."

"Who cares what they think. Gran's house is a few blocks down, take a left."

On a rise, Daisy's grandmother's 1930's two-story house looked every board foot of its eighty-plus years. Painted a dingy gray, with white trim, a good rain or hosing down would brighten its outlook. There were plastic kids' toys strewn all over the porch and dry, yellow lawn. The restraining wall had a crack like a chasm and one section leaned forward.

Rich pulled into the rutted driveway behind Daisy's Korean sedan. Parked on cinder blocks, another vehicle sat before the single car garage.

"Thanks, Boss." Daisy bounded out of the truck toting the
plastic garbage bag of her stuff.

"How do I get to the hospital?"

"Take 72nd south to Dodge. You'll see it." She had to put
all her skinny shoulder into slamming the truck door.

"Thanks," he yelled out, watching her M-65 Field Jacket
climb the porch steps.

Almost hidden behind the gray stone and green glass
towers of the modern Children's Hospital, across from the
heliport, Methodist Hospital Emergency was a throwback, a
small alcove between the main structure and a four-story
parking garage.

Every step tortured Rich as he limped to the emergency
entrance. Outer doors opened. A seated plainclothes security guard reading a newspaper looked up and gave Rich the
once-over.

Rich's smile resembled more of a grimace than a greet-
ing.

The inner doors opened, and Rich made his way to the
reception. A young Hispanic woman sat behind thick Plexiglass, with a circular hole to talk through.

"How can I help you?"

"I need to see a doctor."

"What's the problem?"

"I have a bad cut on my foot and need it looked at."

"Have you been to Methodist before?"

"No."

She started collecting sheets from a stack of trays and putting them on a clipboard. "I will need to see your driver's license. Do you have insurance?"

Rich braced himself on the counter and pulled out his wallet. "No insurance." He handed over his driver's license.

"This is an Illinois license. Do you live in Omaha?"

"I do. I haven't changed over."

"How long have you lived here?"

"About a year, maybe sixteen months. Did I accidentally wander into the DMV?"

The receptionist's face tightened. "No." She glanced at Rich's license. "Mr. Rice. You need to take care of that."

Someone behind the receptionist muttered, "Pita."

"I've been busy. Hey, my mother was a nurse. I'm not a pain in the ass."

The young woman pushed the clipboard through a slot at the bottom of the window. "Fill this out."

A man wearing grimy clothing slept in the corner of the waiting room. A small, green store-bought Christmas tree, with few colored lights, sat crooked on a corner table. Rich eased himself down to a plastic formed chair. The usual forms of past ailments and conditions. On the address line, Rich hesitated. He'd been underground, off-the-grid for a long time, and had never given out his address. Did it matter now? The Russians had killed his wife, and he'd killed them. He scribbled the address for The Ordinary not too legibly.

The receptionist took the clipboard without looking at Rich. She returned the Visa cards and Rich's license. "We'll bill you the charges for your visit."

"Thanks." Rich turned, hobbling back to the waiting room.

Double doors behind him opened.

"Richard Rice," an older woman in blue hospital scrubs called out.

"Right here." It took Rich three moves to completely turn around.

"Got a bad wheel?"

"I guess you could say that."

"Follow me." She pointed to a short row of seats in a narrow hallway. "Have a seat there."

Rich let himself down. His foot throbbed.

A sign on the opposite wall read: WARNING. It is a felony to attack or fight with emergency room personnel. Violators will be arrested and prosecuted to the fullest extent of the law.

The emergency room wore a thick rumpled coat of off-white enamel paint. In spots, the chipped paint revealed a past of robin's egg blue, before that seafoam green, and before that canary yellow. It smelled of iodoform, alcohol wipes, sick, rotted food and unclean people. He couldn't figure out which was worse, the stink of the hospital or the pain of his foot.

"Mr. Rice," said another nurse, coming around a corner. "Follow me to the exam room."

He struggled up.

"Can you make it?"

"Yeah...yeah."

Rich sat on the examining chair. The nurse handed him a hospital gown, then wrapped a blood pressure band around his upper arm.

"I'm not taking my clothes off."

"Standard procedure," she said, pumping up the blood pressure band. "Where's your injury?"

"My foot," he pointed. "And I'm not going Code Blue on you guys."

The nurse let the air out of the band. "Okay." She took his temperature and clipped a wired-in sensor on his finger. An electronic unit on the wall beeped. "Can you take your trousers off?"

"Not easily. Rich's mobile phone buzzed. He pulled it out of his pocket and checked the number. It was a 402.

"Who's calling?"

The nurse pulled out a shelf resting Rich's leg on it and rolling up his pants cuff.

Rich flinched.

"Hurts?"

"Yeah."

"Can you take off your boot?"

"Not easily."

"I can cut the boot."

"I'd rather you not."

"Okay. Hang on." The nurse unlaced Rich's hiking boot and eased it off, heel first.

Rich's sock was clean, but the bottom had a stain.

"Mr. Rice? Richard Rice? It's Detective Forester, Omaha P.D."

"Yeah, detective."

"We'd like you to come down. We've some leads in the investigation on the murder of your wife."

"You do?" Rich replied, with no emotion in his voice.

"We've gathered a lot of evidence and have suspects. Can you come downtown?"

"When?"

"Heck, sooner the better. How about now?"

The nurse prepped a stainless-steel tray on rollers, covering it with a blue cloth. "The doctor will be in shortly," she said and left.

"No can do. I'm at Methodist Hospital."

"What happened?" There seemed too much interest in the detective's tone.

Rich paused and kept his cool. "Long story. How about this afternoon?"

"Sure. Round three?"

"Where?"

"Down at Central."

"Okay. See you then."

There was a knock on the door.

A middle-aged man, also wearing blue scrubs, walked in.

Round, Rich observed, round bald head, round cheeks, round chin, round belly, and short.

"I'm Doctor Bednarik." They shook hands.

He had an impatient manner and peevish blue eyes. The doctor slid a stool over and straddled it. "So, you got a bum paw?"

"My left foot. I got it stitched, but it's really painful and I am worried about infection."

"Well, let's take a look."

Rich winced.

"Hurts?"

The doctor waved his hand. "Whew. What's that smell like to you?"

"Ammonia."

"Yup. Not good." The doctor snapped on a pair of blue rubber gloves and cut away Rich's sock. He moved the tray of instruments over, then cut away the bandage. "You going to tell me what happened?"

"Got a bad cut."

The doctor pulled away the dirty bandage. "How long ago?" He threw it into a covered receptacle.

"Three days, I think."

"You think?" the doctor mocked. He raised Rich's foot by the big toe and examined the bottom. "What the hell? This is nylon fishing line? Who did this?"

Rich jumped when the doctor moved his foot. "Samir, the cousin of my driver."

"He a doctor, or a fishing buddy?"

"Pharmacist."

"Pharmacist?" Doctor Bednarik rolled back to a row of cabinets and pulled a mirror from a drawer. He slid forward and held it for Rich. "Can you see that?"

"Yeah."

"The sutures are uneven. He did stitch from the center out, but they are too far apart. See the redness on the edges and that ooze? That's the smell."

"Uh-huh."

"I'm going to have to open this up, irrigate it and re-suture it a lot tighter than your Pharmacist Sammy. When was your last tetanus shot?'

"No idea. Couple of years ago."

"You're getting another one." The doctor, with tweezers in one hand and snips in the other, started cutting the nylon stitches and pulling them out.

Rich flinched.

"You feeling this? I'm going to shoot numbing stuff around the wound." He prepped a hypodermic needle. "You know," he said, probably to take Rich's mind off the needle. "Pharmacists aren't supposed to do this sort of thing. Where's this Sam-guy from?"

Rich hesitated, considering a reply. "Samir...in India."

The doctor adjusted an overhead light. "Indiana? A little stick."

"No, India." The needle wasn't that bad.

"What?" Doctor Bednarik rolled back on his stool. "India. India? When did you get back?"

"Last night."

The doctor put the hypodermic on the tray. "I assume you got all your shots and took your malaria pills...right?"

"Yeah, Doc. You don't need to worry."

"What were you doing there?"

"Sightseeing."

The doctor grunted. With a folded towel under Rich's heel, he sprayed the wound from a small plastic dispenser, then wiped down the bottom of Rich's foot with gauze. "Tell me how this happened?"

"A cut."

"How?" The doctor picked up a small clamp with a pre-threaded needle.

"Stepped on glass."

Doctor Bednarik glanced up. "Glass, huh? This wound is as straight and deep as the path of a bullet."

Rich did not reply.

"What do you do for a living, Mr. Rice?"

"I own a bar in South Omaha."

"Owns a bar in South Omaha," the doctor grumbled as he worked.

They didn't speak for a long while as the doctor finished stitching and dressing the wound.

"Okay, Mr. Rice," the doctor finally said, slapping his hands on his thighs. "That's about all I can do. It's stitched better." He stood, pulling off his gloves and dropping them in the receptacle. "A nurse will come in and give you a tetanus shot. Leave the bandage on. Don't get it wet. After ten days or two weeks, your doctor can take the stitches out." Folding his arms, he leaned against the cabinets. "Instead of a cam walker, we're giving you a hard-soled surgery shoe. You'll be able to get around better. Wear it for three weeks or until you can put weight on the foot." He stared sternly at Rich. "Welcome back from India. Watch out for broken glass." Then he winked.

"Thanks, Doc."

The doctor walked out, and a nurse came in shortly after. She fitted his foot with the black Velcro-closed shoe, then gave him a tetanus shot in his arm.

"No allergies, right?" the nurse asked.

"None."

She handed him two scrips. "These are for antibiotics for the infection. Take after eating. And the other is tramadol for pain."

"Can I get some Vicodin?"

She looked at him with no expression. "No."

"Just thought I'd ask."

Walking in the hard-soled shoe, plus the local anesthetic helped Rich walk.

On the drive back to The Ordinary, Rich called his lawyer.

"Douglas Borodavka."

"Doug, this is Rich Rice."

"Rich. When did you get back?"

He put the phone on speaker and held it as he drove. "Last night. Listen, the cops want a meetup."

"About your wife's murder? When?"

"Today, at three. Maybe you should be there?"

"I'm in court all day. But I don't think you'll need me."

"Good. There's a bunch of crap coming down with my wife's estate. She's being sued."

"Sued? She's, um, gone. What do they think they'll get?"

"No idea. Can we meet later, after you're done with court?"

"Sure, around dinner time? Is Jorge on the grill?"

Rich smiled and rolled his eyes. "Yeah. Come on over to The Ordinary."

"I'd be delighted."

CHAPTER 3

A dreary day, under low sky and drizzle. Not cold enough to ice over, nor warm enough to evaporate, the cars plowed through slush on wet streets.

Rich pumped quarters into a parking meter until it burped.

The hard-soled shoe made walking less painful, less laborious as Rich crossed 15th Street.

He surveyed the Omaha Police headquarters building and wondered if the architect had been seduced by the voice of a beehive. The segmented block style resembled a concrete honeycomb.

Crossing the concourse, Rich remembered the last time he was there, reporting Gisele a missing person.

He went through the metal detector without a beep, having left his concealed carry tucked under the driver's seat.

A silver tinsel tree, tucked in a far corner, flashed blue and red lights. Two large toy drive boxes flanked the display.

"I'm here to see Detective Forester."

"I'll need to see your driver's license," said a young blonde woman, with droopy eyes, wearing a tight blue uniform with no rank and no badge. She stood behind a high counter nearly dwarfed by a bank of computers.

"Will my passport do?"

"Sure. Most people just show their driver's license."

Rich handed over his blue-jacketed passport. "It's easier if I use my passport."

She keyed information into a computer then slid a Visitor badge across the counter. Idly, she leafed through Rich's passport. "You've been to some places."

Rich made her jump, reaching over the counter and snatching his passport from her hands. "Haven't I, though?"

Shaken, the young woman said, "Detective Forester is on the fourth floor. He'll meet you at the elevator."

"Thanks."

The elevator doors parted. Rich stepped out into a hallway that divided two office areas. No one met him. He turned and checked the number over the elevator. Four.

On one side, a long corridor led to a large room with mismatched beige and gray cubicles. Plainclothes and uniformed officers bustled about the noisy area. It didn't resemble a standard police squad room. A mess of papers piled here and there and pasted to the walls, people talking on the phone and the conversations reminded Rich more like a newspaper newsroom.

He unbuttoned his heavy wool Navy pea coat and peeked into the other side. This area had offices and glassed conference rooms and was incredibly quiet.

Rich recognized the thin-haired and older Detective Forester walking briskly toward him. He wore tan business slacks, a blue dress shirt and gray sweater vest, with a glint of silver clipped to his belt. Forester had files, a laptop and a bulky package under one arm. He held out his free hand to Rich.

"Mr. Rice, thanks for coming down." His deeply lined face seemed to sag with fatigue.

They shook hands.

"Not a problem." Forester's hand was cold and wet.

"Follow me," the detective said. "We've got a conference room scheduled." He walked with his head cocked upward, reading numbers over glass doors. "Not sure which...ah, here it is." He stepped back to let Rich enter first.

A large, highly polished brown table just about filled the narrow room. To the left of the head of the table sat another man before an open laptop. He was dressed similarly to Forester and looked familiar.

"You remember Detective Lyons?"

The man sniffled and scrubbed his index finger several times under his nose. He offered Rich a casual wave.

Rich remembered him. "How are you detective?"

"Fighting a cold."

Rich paused, waiting for Forester to pick a side of the table. (He slipped left, sitting near Lyons.) Rich circled right to the middle of the table, across from Forester.

Forester sat and jumped his chair closer to the table. "They patch you up? What happened?"

Rich draped his coat over the back of the padded pleather chair and pushed up the sleeves of his black cashmere sweater. "Just a boo boo." He eased himself into the chair.

"Detective Lyons will be transcribing our meeting into the Case Management System. That's so CIB can evaluate the progress."

"CIB?"

"Criminal Investigations Bureau. They have functional control over all active cases. The homicide of your wife is an active case. But..."

"But?"

The detective took a breath. "We've sort of slowed down and CIB thought bringing you in and having a talk could push us in the right direction."

"I gave you statements and everything I can think of. Not sure how I can help."

Lyons sneezed into cupped hands and wiped them down his pants, then went back to typing.

"Then you were gone for ten days."

Rich tensed, leaning back in his chair. "Yeah, so?"

"Nobody at The Ordinary knew where you were or if you were coming back."

"It wasn't their concern."

"Borodavka, your lawyer, didn't have a clue."

"Nor is it your concern."

"Listen." Forester looked over at Lyons. "Stop typing, Fred. And go get some tissues."

Fred pulled his hands back from the keyboard. "I'm okay."

"If it didn't happen in my Metro, I don't give a rat's." Forester slouched forward and folded his hands. "Throughout our investigation, we've been getting these hints and rumors and comments from the Feds and international sources. I don't just mean CIA and State Department. There's a couple of foreign governments that have sent us inquiries about you."

"And what did you do?"

"Way beyond my pay grade. Truth is we don't know what we got."

Rich glanced down, thought a moment. His head came up. His hard stare must've startled Forester because he fidgeted. "Detective, I am not going to talk about certain things. But after we talk, you might have a better overall picture."

"We appreciate that."

Fred's hands went to the keyboard.

"Not yet, Fred," Rich said. "What I want to know is why the Feds aren't leading this investigation."

"Our question also. Especially with the suspects involved being foreign nationals and the evidence we've uncovered."

"Why would they just drop it into your lap?"

"Don't know." Forester fell back in his chair. "Maybe they want to keep it local to hold the stink down. Maybe they thought you'd be more willing to cooperate with us than with them."

"I am willing to cooperate...to a point."

Forester screwed up his face and looked sideways at Rich. "I gotta say, most guys would be banging the table, yelling at us to find the killers of their wife. But you...you're as cool as the other side of the pillow."

Rich regarded Forester for a long time. Lyons and Forester nervously traded glances.

Low and slow, Rich said, "Show me what you got on the killers of my wife, Detective."

"Okay," Forester shrugged, sitting up. "Close the computer, Fred."

"I hate typing anyway."

"You understand there are things we can't show you. They may be used later as evidence in court. As it is, we are going way beyond SOP just showing you this."

"Show me. Understand, I can only help you so much."

"Just keep us from spinning our wheels," Forester muttered as he brought out an HDMI line and plugged it from his laptop to a projector on the table. The fan loudly hissed when he pressed the power button. "Remind me never to play poker with you, Mr. Rice."

"I'm a terrible poker player."

A desktop with files and apps materialized on the wall behind the conference table. Lyons got up and turned off the lights. Forester clicked on a file.

"You going to be okay seeing this?"

"Don't worry about me."

"If what happened to your wife, happened to my wife, I'd be shattered."

"I'm still putting the pieces back together."

"Understood."

Forester clicked on a numbered file with titled photos and minimized it. Then he clicked another file called videos. A gray and black picture came up, with a white type date stamp and start arrow in the center. He clicked on it.

"We spliced together CCTV footage from various sources. This is from a camera on the second floor of the building next door to Prince Fong's on 16th Street."

A black Honda Accord angled into a parking spot. A tall woman, slender and stylishly dressed, climbed out of the car.

"That's..." the detective started.

"My wife." Rich finished.

Seeing Gisele, Rich almost doubled over as if a P72 Louisville Slugger caught him mid-swing right in the gut. He tried to tackle his leaping heart. He struggled to breathe.

He must've worn a stricken face; concern deepened the furrows across Forester's forehead.

"You all right?" Forester paused the video.

Rich held his hand up.

Lyons looked over his shoulder at him.

"Give me a second." He finally caught his breath. "I didn't think it, didn't think, it would affect me like that."

"You're human, after all. I told you if it had been my wife..." The detective waited.

The ache turned to a sensation of being buried down deep in a black hole, with no way to climb out. In a moment, he was able to pull himself together.

"Okay. Go ahead."

"This is in front of your lawyer's office." He set the video in motion.

"I told her to go. They sent her a fake subpoena. Why the hell...?"

"Get her alone, isolated."

Gisele slid her credit card into the parking meter then crossed the sidewalk, disappearing from view.

"Presumably, she goes up to your lawyer's office. Here's where it gets hinky."

A gray, four-door sedan parked behind Gisele's Honda. The video quality pixilated, but a driver and front-seat passenger could be made out.

"I am going to fast forward here," and the detective sped through the video.

Gisele appeared on the sidewalk. Forester stopped and let the video roll at normal speed. She went around the front of her car, clicking the fob to open the door. As she pulled open the driver's door, two men jumped out of the gray sedan, one from the passenger side and another from the back seat on the driver's side.

Rich recognized them right away. A stocky blond man and a lanky, greasy black-haired man wearing a long coat.

Gisele turned to get into her car. The blond rushed her. He grabbed her from behind and pushed an automatic against her back. She fought, punching and kicking at the man. He brought the butt of the automatic down hard on her head. She slumped, seemingly dazed, and he shoved her into the car. The greasy-haired one opened the back door. He brought up a sawed-off shotgun from inside his coat as he slipped in.

The camera angle didn't show much. But a flurry of movement visible through the windshield meant Gisele continued to fight.

Rich wanted to cry out. He would have if he wasn't so goddamn angry.

"We got a 911 call about an abduction. A patrol car was on the scene in minutes but didn't find anything."

They seemed to subdue Gisele and the Accord pulled out onto 16th Street. The gray sedan followed nearly on its bumper.

"Who's driving that car?"

"We think the stout guy is in the front, and the skinny guy is in back with a shotgun on your wife."

"No, the car following them?" Rich pointed, nearly shouting.

"We got a pretty good idea."

"There were more of them?"

"Looks that way." The detective minimized the video and clicked open a photo file.

More? Rich thought. I got only two of them. There's more.

An enlarged passport photo of the blond man filled the wall. He had a broad face with a confused expression.

"This is Sklyar Misko. Ukrainian by birth, from the Privoz area of Odessa. His criminal record is fairly standard for these types. Started out a street rat committing petty theft, purse snatching, mugging, pickpocket, extortion. One mugging gone bad when he was a teenager got him a stretch in Lustdorf Prison. The first of many. That's where he was recruited by the *Vory* and eventually muscle for the Franko Family. He's known for being ruthless, and particularly cold-blooded, but as dumb as a bowl of Borscht."

Rich remembered hiding in the shadows that night behind the KGB Villa in India, with only a knife. Misko came around the side with an automatic ready. Rich jumped him and they grappled. Misko lost the automatic but tumbled Rich. He leapt to his feet and plunged the blade just under the man's rib cage. Warm blood spurted over Rich's hand and wrist.

"Misko was at the Grand Jury hearing in Omaha," Rich said.

The detective clicked through photos of Misko. "Yeah, we got him there too." He added, "Passport Control has him flying out of Omaha that night, then connecting to a flight to St. Petersburg."

"What about the other one?"

"The one with the shotgun? He was on the same flight."

"No. What's his name?"

"Gotcha." Forester closed Misko's file and opened a second. A grainy picture of a skinny, bony faced, longish haired man showed on the wall.

"This little beauty is Razvan Negrescu. He's Romanian from Navodari, north of Constanta. His mother is originally from Greece, Serbian blood. He worked as a fisherman on the Black Sea but turned to smuggling, a more lucrative gig. He robbed NATO stores and ran American cigarettes and liquor between Romania and Odessa. Nikoli Franko recruited him for the family's Eastern European human trafficking operation."

Negrescu had recognized Rich disguised as a beggar outside the Villa and went for an automatic inside his down vest. Rich had luck, and was quicker, jamming a Tazer into the Romanian's throat. He lay unconscious as Rich looped a thick zip tie binding the man's wrists, ankles and finally one around his neck, tightly cinching it around his neck. He never took another breath.

"We got information on this guy from EU law enforcement and an Interpol office in Turkey."

"What about the gray car?" Rich wanted to know. "The others?"

"We don't see him for a while. I want to pick it up from 16th street and Farnum." Forester minimized and opened the video file. Another video showed the two cars going through an intersection. "This is off a stoplight camera. They stayed on 16th to Dodge, then right on Capitol and left on 16th Street. It's all surface streets, with factories and residential areas."

Rich hardly heard the detective. All he thought about was there was a third man. He hadn't known about him.

He had missed one.

Who was he?

"They must've scouted the route because 16th sort of dead ends at Read. The road jogs to the left and merges onto JJ Pershing." The captured CCTV video jumped. "OPPD's North Omaha Power Plant. Note the time stamp—4:45 PM. The next time we see them, it's 7:10, nearly dusk. This video is from the front gate of the Missouri River Project."

"We don't have any idea what happened for two and a half hours," Lyons said with a snort.

Forester picked a sheet of paper from the file folder. "This is the autopsy report on your wife. Did you see this?" The detective's eyes flicked across at Rich.

"No."

"She had bruising all over her arms and shoulders, as well as legs, belly and back. You can have this." He waved the report.

"No."

Awkwardly, Forester returned the report to the file. "I'm not, I'm not, going to read any more of this." He turned away from Rich. "We can pick up the video trail and ah, assume they stopped someplace, maybe under the Mormon Bridge for a while."

"I think they ran that stop sign, John."

"Wouldn't be surprised."

The cars sped past NP Dodge Park.

"We don't see them again until they pull into the Hummel Park Nature Center."

Both cars parked.

Lyons waved to Forester to stop the video. "There's a part here that may be difficult for him."

"I can take it."

Forester started up the black and white video. The room grew quiet, as all three stared at the screen. A white flash lit up the inside of Gisele's Accord. The front passenger window exploded out with small bits glittering in the light.

"Run it again."

"Are you sure?"

"Yes."

"You know what that is?" Forester's tone sounded hesitant.

"Run it again," Rich's voice rose.

Forester reversed and ran the video.

A flash and then explosion out the front.

"RUN IT AGAIN," he screamed. His fists clenched on the tabletop.

Lyons' eyes slid over to Forester. The detective shrugged.

A flash. It was Negrescu from the back seat with the shotgun. An outward explosion. He'd killed Gisele. Rich had killed him. For an instant, he was satisfied.

"Let it run."

After a moment, a figure emerged from the second car and came around to the Accord.

"Who's this?" Rich stood.

"From the following car. The other guy."

"The third man?" Rich went to the screen.

"That's a rental car, rented at the airport. We got a name. Symon Roitman."

Rich studied the blurry image. He was thick and not overly muscular, wearing a dark tracksuit jacket. His square-shaped head had a stubble cut. A hand went to his flat face, then a large cloud blew out his mouth.

"He's vaping."

"Roitman is German/Russian, second generation. His grandfather was Schutz Staffel, the SS, occupying lower Russia. He's well educated. Graduate of Patrice Lumumba University in Moscow. Currently, he's some kind of go-fer for Ukrainian/Jewish real estate mogul Boyko Nudelman." Forester shuffled through papers. "This Nudelman character is a real piece of work."

"I know about Nudelman," Rich interrupted. "I've been writing about these guys for years. Can you make the picture of Roitman bigger?"

"Sorry, can't."

Rich squinted at the projected features. "Does he have a cleft lip?"

"A hare-lip? Yeah." Lyons laughed and coughed. "Had, though. Thanks to some crappy Commie Doc, he ended up with a wide, dark scar from lip to nostril."

"He gave a San Diego address," Forester added. "Doesn't make sense. The other two are foreign nationals."

"What's his San Diego address?"

"Can't give you that."

Rich half-shrugged. "Doesn't matter." And returned to the chair. He scribbled something in his notebook.

The video ran, showing the three men pull a woman's naked body out of the front passenger side. Half of the woman's face had been blown off. Her shoulders were discolored, and fluid streamed onto the ground.

Seized with anger, Rich watched as they carried the body up wooden steps on a hillside trail into the trees. For an instant, he thought it wasn't really Gisele. But he saw the musical staff and lyrics tattooed on her shoulder.

The children of tomorrow/Share their dreams
With you and me
Take me to the magic of the moment/On a glory night.
He knew.

Forester closed the file. The projector fan hissed. They sat in the half-dark, not saying a word.

"So, Mr. Rice," the detective finally spoke up. "That's where we're at. We have three suspects. Two foreign nationals, and some mystery dude from San Diego." Forester slapped the folder closed. "We have questions for you. Where were you the last ten days?"

Rich slowly drummed his fingers on the table and eyed Forester across the polished wood. The detective's expression reflected his question.

"Not telling?"

"Don't have to."

"We can figure it out from the inquiries sent about you from foreign police agencies."

"Well, there you go."

"FBI is giving us squat. And some agency higher than the FBI is stonewalling us. But the State Department, the frickin' State Department, has sent an inquiry. So I'm asking you. We know something happened. We want to know what."

Rich swayed back, rocking in the pleather chair. He exhaled. "Don't dick around with those two. The only one you need concern yourself with finding is the third guy, the driver of the second car...Roitman."

The detectives traded looks.

"I told you Misko and Negrescu hopped a flight to St. Petersburg, Russia," Forester said with a twisted mouth. "But Roitman didn't turn in the rental car until days later. Did you get that tingling on the back of your neck? That nagging sensation of being shadowed?"

"Why?"

Forester opened and fast-forwarded to another video. "This might clue you in." He let the video play. He seemed to enjoy cautioning Rich. The image of Roitman came out of the shadows crossing a street.

"Where is that?"

Roitman stopped on the sidewalk. A vape pen dangled from his lips.

Rich recognized the street. "How'd you get that?"

"We pulled your surveillance video at The Ordinary."

"*Tipo Malo*," Rich muttered, remembering Jorge's comment. "With dead eyes."

"What's that?"

"I asked my cook if anyone had been asking for me. He said *Tipo Malo*."

"Bad dude, huh," Forester replied. "He got that right."

Lyons hacked into a loose fist and went to the door.

"How'd you I.D. those guys so quickly?"

"We're good," Lyons sniffed and said. "They used their real names and left a lot of evidence at the crime scene."

"If your intent is reprisal it's pointless to conceal it."

"True. Honestly, we're not as good as Fred says." Forester pinched a paper out of a folder. "They really didn't do much to disguise who they were and what they did. Roitman flew in a day early." Forester scanned the sheet and paraphrased. "He rented a car and two mid-priced rooms at the Doubletree downtown. He's a resident alien and registered as such. Roitman picked up the other two at Eppley. Being foreign nationals, they had to use their Russian passports. Misko and Negrescu bunked in one room. Roitman had a room to himself. Cleaning lady said one room didn't appear it was slept in, while the other was littered with beer cans and vodka bottles."

"That cheap vodka in plastic gallon jugs," Lyons snapped on the lights.

"They ate twice at an Indian restaurant and the usual fast food joints. Roitman used a credit card, which is not too bright."

"And the weapons?" Rich asked. "They couldn't have carried them in."

"I dunno. Might've been disassembled in check bags?" Lyons slipped behind Forester, returning to his seat.

"No. We know they bought a shotgun at Walmart. The one down I-80, in Gretna. Walk in, fill out a form, and walk out with a shotgun and box of shells."

"Chinese model, plastic stock, real crap."

"And a hacksaw. You think that might've clued someone."

"The automatic?" Rich pressed.

"Pawnshop or gun show in Iowa," Forester said. "We know the three of them drove out to a titty bar in Carter Lake. Couple of the girls remember obnoxious foreign guys on the rail. We checked, there was a gun show in Council Bluffs that same day."

"Did you recover the weapons?'

"More than likely, they're at the bottom of the Missouri River."

"Cell phone records?"

"Not a chance. Feds are sitting on a subpoena."

"They must've had blood spatter all over their clothes. You find any?"

"Nope. Hotel staff complained they stole all the towels. They probably deep-sixed the laundry as well."

"Got warrants ready?"

"Yup. Fat lot of good that does us. Bureaucratic red tape and the fact we don't have an extradition treaty with the Russians makes the two that fucked off to Putin-ville virtually untouchable."

"What about you?" Lyons said.

"You have everything you need to know."

"Don't forget—this is in my Metro."

"You've been square with me. You went way over the line and showed me things I know you wouldn't have shared with someone—who might be a suspect themself." Rich closed his notebook and stood. "I appreciate that. I'll give you a statement. It'll fill in some blanks." He hooked the collar of his coat and pulled it off the chair back.

"Do it now." Forester dared him, the vein up his neck swelling.

"It's not over." Rich moved to the door.

"Dammit, Mr. Rice..." Forester rose angrily, banging his chair against the wall. "Don't be a vigilante. You're not cut out for it."

"Maybe not." Rich had his hand on the doorknob. "But I'm learning, learning real fast." He opened the door.

"I can have you arrested." Red-faced, Forester chased after Rich out the door.

"On what charge?" Rich slipped on his coat and pushed the elevator button.

"Stupidity, and it would stick. You're going to get yourself killed," the detective shouted from the hallway.

Rich glanced over, smiled and nodded, stepping into the elevator.

CHAPTER 4

A half-hour after Rich returned to The Ordinary, his large, wild-haired and bearded lawyer, entered with a splay-footed waddle.

Rich met him at the bar. "Let's get a booth."

Borodavka looked rumpled and weary. His cranberry-colored suit hung as tired on his body as the bags under his eyes. He set his leather briefcase in the corner and brought his bulk to the padded seat.

"Long day in court?" Rich slid into the booth across from Borodavka.

"Don't ask." The lawyer unclasped his case and brought out a hefty pile of folders and papers.

At the bar, Riku and Daisy sorted through green garland and tangled strands of tiny colored lights in a battered cardboard beer box. Rich waved and caught Daisy's attention. She came right over.

"Thanks, Daisy." He glanced at Borodavka who sorted through papers. "You want anything to drink?"

"Yes," he said with a sigh. "Don't mind if I do. A Bud Light."

"You want something, Boss?"

"Club soda."

"Make mine two," Borodavka added.

"Excuse me?" Daisy asked.

"Two Bud Lights."

"Ohhhh-kay." Daisy half-turned and gave Rich a 'what the?' face.

"And ask Jorge to come here. I'm sure Mr. Borodavka is hungry after a long day litigating."

"Yes, indeed."

Daisy returned to the bar.

Borodavka held up a bulky white 8 by 10 envelope. "You want this back?"

"What is it?"

"You gave this envelope to me before you left. I don't think you thought you were coming back."

Rich wiped his hand across his mouth, a thoughtful gesture. "You're right about that. Maybe you should keep it."

Borodavka tucked the envelope into his case, just as Jorge came out of the kitchen.

"*Jefe*, Daisy say you want me?" The cook's hair was tucked under a puffy white elastic band cap. He wore a clean knee-length apron.

"Mr. Borodavka is hungry."

"Ahhhh, Chef Ruiz, good to see you."

With a quick sideways look at Rich, Jorge offered the big man a false smile.

"*Si...si.*"

"I want three enchiladas, two beef, one chicken..."

Rich detached himself, staring out the dark window. Car headlights and red taillights crisscrossed on the glass. Indistinct voices from shadows moved along the sidewalk. He glanced around the barroom at people laughing, drinking, and the regulars along the bar, bending elbows.

Out of the bar speakers, a slow guitar played. A world-weary voice sang: *Sometimes I don't know where this dirty road is taking me. Sometimes I can't even see the reason why. I guess I'll keep a'gamblin'; lots of booze and lots of ramblin'—it's easier than just waitin' around to die.*

He had a sensation of being extremely far away.

"...and then for dessert two scoops of vanilla ice cream with strawberry sauce."

"*Jefe?*"

Rich came back. "Yeah? What's up?"

Jorge wore a tortured look on his face. "He want *helado?*"

"We don't have any...right?"

"This a *taberna*, not a *Lecheria* Queen. You go get a snowstorm you self."

"Oh, that's sad. Maybe a shot of Patron for dessert."

"You ask Daisy for that. I bring you plate when all set."

Jorge could not get back to the safety of his kitchen fast enough.

"What happened at the cops?"

"A lot," Rich looked down at his hands. "I don't want to talk about that now."

"What then? Your wife's situation?"

"Yeah, her being sued."

"I am not a stock or financial attorney," Borodavka said. "I have a couple of interns who specialize in this type of law. I can bring them in."

"I don't really know what it's all about. It's something my mother-in-law said."

Daisy appeared with a round tray and placed two Bud Lights before the large lawyer, and a club soda by Rich's left hand.

Borodavka's eyes roved over her.

"Thanks, Daisy."

"I've got a fair idea what's going on. Your wife had a stockbroker business, right?"

"Yeah. She had about two dozen clients. They decided to stay with her even after she came to live with me in Omaha."

"She that good?" The lawyer tipped back a beer.

"She was. She wanted out, but they persuaded her to administer their accounts until they could move them," Rich paused. "She had a really good eye for future trends. Her clients were in Amazon early and lately Canadian cannabis companies."

"Since she was murdered a month ago..."

"Three weeks and three days," Rich corrected.

"Okay," Borodavka bowed, his hands out. "They may be suing to regain control of their accounts and move them to where they want. You'll need the death certificate and something that verifies you have power of attorney."

"Makes sense."

"Probably stipulated in her will. I can help you with that." Borodavka had his bottle poised and ready. "Let me know when you get a copy of your wife's will from her mother." He drained the beer. "Ahhhh."

"Don't know what else is going on out there. I plan to drive out."

A bell rang in the kitchen.

"Hope that's for me."

Daisy ducked into the kitchen and came out with a tray. She turned toward the booth.

"All right," Borodavka gleefully rubbed his hairy hands together.

Daisy served. "I guess this is all for him. Careful, hot plate."

Borodavka grabbed his utensils and surrounded the plate as might a dog with a prized meaty bone.

Fragrant steam came off the red sauce and cheese smothering the cozy trio of enchiladas, buttressed by a mound of rice and black beans.

"Have you eaten today, Boss?"

"Yeah."

"What?"

"I don't recall. I'm fine. Thanks."

"Want to talk about the cops now?" Borodavka said, stuffing his mouth.

Rich took a drink of club soda and turned to the window. A clatter of silverware and china sounded across the table. He remembered the CCTV footage of Gisele.

"Gonna tell me?" The lawyer washed down his food with a long pull on his second beer.

Exhaling, toying with the club soda glass, turning it round and round, Rich considered what to say.

"Detective Forster and his partner Lyons brought me up-to-date on their investigation and the status of finding the murderers of my wife. They showed me a closed-circuit video of Gisele being snatched and...." His voice trailed off.

"They have suspects?"

"Yeah. Those two dudes we saw at the grand jury hearing."

"Them, I remember."

"But there's a third guy I didn't know about."

"That a good thing?"

"Bad thing for him."

"They got warrants? Any leads where to arrest'em?" Borodavka raised his empty bottle toward the bar and gave it a wiggle.

"Two were foreign nationals and they flew back to Russia after killing Gisele. The third one is a problem. He gave a San Diego address and may still be in the US."

"Two left the country?" The lawyer finished the enchiladas and dug into the beans and rice. "Didn't you?"

Rich squinted at Borodavka, noticing rice and red sauce in the man's wild beard. "We have lawyer/client privilege?"

"Yupper."

Daisy swung by and put down a fresh beer. "Are you done with those?"

"Yeah. You can take'em."

Borodavka watched her leave.

Rich waited until Daisy was out of earshot. "Those two? They're nothing to worry about."

"Which means?"

"Means they're nothing to worry about."

"Gotcha."

"This third man. A problem. He'll be dealt with."

Borodavka's pudgy hand went up and his eyes wrinkled with concern. "Whoa...whoa...Mr. Rice...Rich...if that means what I think it does, I don't want to hear it. And I caution you to let the police handle it."

Rich tilted his head and gave his lawyer a sideways smile. "Clean yourself up." He handed across a paper napkin. "Remember who you work for."

Borodavka took the napkin and wiped his mouth, beard and shirt front. "I work for you."

"You do. I need you to bone up on extradition and any treaties the US may have with..."

"Extradition?" the lawyer balled up the napkin and carefully laid it on the table. "With what country?"

"Countries. I don't think we have extradition treaties with the Russian Federation or the Ukraine. Wouldn't prevent them from demanding I be handed over."

"No, you're right. But why..." Borodavka spoke slowly, not understanding. "would they want you?"

"A misunderstanding." He couldn't resist it. "A misunderstanding with an MP-443 Grach."

"I don't want to hear this."

"I'm pretty sure we have extradition with India. You will need to fight that tooth and nail."

"India? Russia? What did you do?"

"Thought you didn't want to know?"

Borodavka stroked his full beard. "You're right. I don't." He combed his fingers through the curly nest of hair. Then stopped. "What do the cops know?"

"Not much. They're not stupid, though." Rich finished his club soda. "Not stupid at all. If they're getting inquiries from foreign governments and international law enforcement agencies, it's not for giving a one-legged beggar a hundred rupees."

Borodavka raised his beer. "I know about extradition from my immigration cases. First, were you convicted of a crime?"

"No."

"So you are not now a fugitive?"

"No. I may be wanted in India as the subject in the investigation of a crime."

"A capital crime?"

"Something you don't want to hear."

"I assume it is, and you'd be the target of the investigation."

"No doubt."

"If you are indeed a target, a person of interest, whatever you want to call it, either at present or soon Interpol will issue a Red Notice. It's an international 'look-out'—like a warrant."

Daisy came up with another beer. The lawyer gave her a big, hairy smile.

Rich held a hand up before his lawyer.

"India," he continued as she left. "through their embassy via the Secretary of State could ask for you to be handed over. State would review the case, then forward it to the Criminal Division's Office of International Affairs—the OIA. State could issue a surrender warrant."

"The U.S. extradites its citizens to other countries?"

"Depends on the crime." Borodavka drank. "And the treaty."

"I'm fucked."

The big man drew his sleeve across his beer-wet mouth. "Lures and snatches."

"Snatches? Lures?"

"You'll have to be alert. It's a common thing. If there is no treaty, like the U.S. and Russia, some national police agencies, try to lure an extradition target out of their safe haven to another country that has an extradition treaty. Then they request arrest and extradition."

"Do India and Russia have a treaty?"

"I'd bet my three little smiling Borodavkas on it."

"You'll have to fight like hell."

"There are ways around it."

"Like what?"

"Some countries, U.S. is one, won't extradite to countries if they have the death penalty or a history of torture. Or, for political reasons." He finished the beer. "You could also get a second passport."

"Say again?" Rich leaned across the table.

"A second passport. There are countries that will issue you a passport even though you hold a U.S. passport."

"What does that take?"

"Ancestry, time...and, of course, money."

"And, if I have documents with another identity I could, from one of these countries, get a passport in that name."

"In ten days to two weeks.

"You know of these countries?"

"Usual suspects, Bermuda, Cayman Islands, Cyprus," the hairy lawyer screwed up his eyes to the ceiling. Prices range from fifteen thousand dollars in Thailand to one million bucks in Australia."

"Too rich for my blood. I'm not moving to Thailand."

"You know, I may have an alternative. I have an address and agent in Panama you could use."

"I'm interested. What'll it cost me?"

"The agent, address and birth certificate would be around ten thousand. The bribe to the government official should be as much as five to another ten thousand. The passport itself is only a couple of hundred."

"How do I pay it—in Balboas?"

Borodavka burst out laughing. "You got any Balboas laying around?"

"No."

"Don't worry. They love Yankee greenbacks."

"Very interested."

"I'll get back to you on it."

"Those were three well-spent enchiladas."

Borodavka threw back his head and laughed. He raised his beer. "To freedom."

"No...to second passports."

CHAPTER 5

"Offh…owwww."

Rich stood aside the booth, watching as his lawyer struggled to get out.

"Must've been that last enchilada."

"Uh-huh," Rich said.

The large man huffed and grunted, scooting inch by inch out between the table and the bench. Finally, Borodavka managed to swing one leg out and then twist around and get his bulk out.

"That should take care of my work-out for the week." The lawyer paused. "Before I go, I want to give you something."

"Oh? My dad warned me about lawyers bearing gifts."

Borodavka fished a business card from his inside pocket and handed it to Rich.

"What's this?"

The card had the imprint Centering Corp—Grief Resource Center and was on Maple Street.

"Don't take this the wrong way, but when I first met you, you were a regular guy caught up in the chaos and confusion of being pursued and getting cornered by the Russian Mafia. Add to that the prospects of facing a grand jury hearing."

Anger simmered inside Rich.

"I liked you and thought you were interesting. But since then, with all that has happened, you've changed. They murdered your wife. Now you're bitter and..." His voice trailed off.

"You'd be as well if they took your wife from you."

"No doubt. But I hope I would be big enough to realize I need help. You've been carrying this for a while and afraid to let go of your rage. I think you believe if you let go and go through the grief, it means you didn't love your wife. That's not the case. I won't say any more about it. They have people at the Center who will listen and let you grieve."

Rich let his anger subside, knowing the lawyer meant only to help him.

Hoots and whistles and a commotion by the door drew Rich's attention.

Two tall girls dressed in tan fringed vests, tan fringed dresses, brown fringed boots, wearing small tan velvet cowboy hats pinned in their long black hair, were surrounded by eager college boys.

"Yumi and Ami," Rich said with a sigh. "I might've known."

"What's going on?"

"Something I need to take care of," Rich started for the front. He turned back, with hand out. "Thanks, Doug. I'll be seeing my mother-in-law this weekend and get the lowdown on the lawsuit."

"Give me a call."

Rich weaved his way across the crowded bar floor. "Excuse me. Excuse me." Then came face to face with the two young women. "Can I talk to you two?"

"Mr. Rice. Certainly."

"Come on, guys—back to your seats."

Ami and Yumi trailed Rich to the POS station at the end of the bar.

"I am sorry that this is how we first meet," Rich began. "And I am just going to jump into it. I don't mind if you two dress alike."

"It's cosplay. Lots of people do it."

"I'm not totally unhip. However, I heard about your Japanese schoolgirl's costumes."

"That was a night." The two girls giggled.

"That night," Rich's voice turned stern. "...will never be repeated...understood?" He paused. "If you want to continue working here."

One girl looked down. The other's face lost its amusement.

"We didn't mean anything by it."

"We thought it would bring in people."

"I understand that. I know I was out of town and no one told you you were dressed inappropriately. I am doing that now." Rich waited a moment. "Nothing provocative. Nothing overtly sexual. Okay?"

"How about what we have on now?"

"Weird, but okay."

"We're sorry, Mr. Rice."

"It won't happen again."

"Good. We won't need to talk about this again. Everything I have heard about you two has been very good. I'd like that to continue."

"It will." One girl ducked under the bar apron. Her sister followed.

Rich looked past the girls, up the bar. "Thanks, girls." He approached a thin, scraggly bearded man wearing a soft newsboy cap. He appeared to be in his early thirties.

"Pay for your beer and get out."

The man swallowed. "What? I'm just enjoying my beer. Chill, dude."

"Riku," Rich called. The Korean came up. "Is this guy running a tab? How much does he owe?"

"He's had three beers."

"Four beers. I saw him reach over and tap that beer."

"Oh, I did not."

They stared at each other.

"Besides, what business is it of yours?"

"Pay for four beers and get out."

"What if I said fuck off."

"I'd say that was a stupid thing to say."

"The owner's rich. He don't care."

Riku's eye fixed on Rich.

"Who told you that?"

"My buddies."

"Your buddies here now?"

"Maybe."

"They can get out also."

The barroom fell silent as people became aware of the altercation at the bar.

"And what if we don't want to?"

"Another stupid move." Rich set his stance, ready for the man's move.

Riku reached under the bar. Rich held out his hand, signaling Riku to keep it under the bar.

"I think I told you to fuck off." The man took another pull at his beer.

"Pay up and get out."

"Why do you care?"

"This is my bar."

The man's expression froze. "Are you the one they call Keeper?"

Rich nodded.

"I'm only paying for three beers."

"You'll pay for four."

He started to swing his leg out from the barstool. Rich caught him at an awkward moment burying his fist into the man's belly just below the sternum. He doubled over—the wind knocked out of him.

"Pay up and get out."

One hand on his gut, the man pulled out his billfold. He picked out a twenty.

"We'll keep the change," Riku said.

"No, give him his change, every last penny."

Riku spilled dollars and coins in the man's grimy hand.

"Your buddies too."

"They ain't here."

Rich walked him out. "Anything happens to my bar I'll know it's you."

Someone was applauding in the bar. "That guy's been doing that for years. No one called him on it. No one until you."

"Thanks," Daisy whispered, passing behind Rich pushing a tray of drinks.

He caught up with her after she had served a table with two older couples. "I'm going to be gone next weekend..."

She gave him an angry look. "Where now?"

The attitude took Rich aback, but he let it go. "I'll be at my mother-in-law's in Glencoe. I should be back in a couple of days."

"Oh, okay," Daisy's expression lost its anger. "Sorry, Boss."

"Not a problem."

"It's Christmas in a couple of weeks."

They stopped at the POS terminal at the end of the bar.

"I'm aware of that."

Riku set out a drink order.

"Just wanted to know if we'd be open or what." Her voice changed. "Where do these go?" she said to Riku.

"Booth three."

Daisy put the drinks on a round tray and crossed the bar to booth three.

Rich merged onto the interstate early, hoping to miss traffic and an impending snowstorm and get to Glencoe by midafternoon.

Patchy snow covered most of Iowa.

He punched around stations on the radio. It annoyed him.

MP3s irritated him. Every song had a memory.

In the end, he settled into silence.

He drove down the low slopes into shallow valleys and up distant rolling ridges. The drone of the engine, the rhythm of the tires and wind against the windshield, let him escape his thoughts.

One minute he was heavy, so heavy and underwater, the next minute he became fire, fire scorching across the sky. Then he was grubby, like dirt, that cool, moist dirt of a deep suffocating grave.

He parked at the cemetery in Skokie and walked in a muddy, slushy rut on the lane to Gisele's gravesite. He pocketed dried up flowers wilted over the sides of a brass vase, then brushed dead leaves and snow off her gravestone. For a long time, he stood, his coat bundled tight against the sharp wind off Lake Michigan.

Lake effect snow had piled up on the hedges and brick walls on either side of Sheridan Street in Glencoe. Rich pulled into the circular drive at Gisele's family home. A forest green two-story Edwardian with L-shaped veranda on the front and side of the house. A plume of white smoke rose out of a pipe end on the high peak of the house's roof.

He parked, stepped out and pulled his black duffel bag behind him.

Frau Esslin opened the front door with a shout. "Richard. I *em zo* happy to see you."

A tiny woman, Rich stooped low to hug her across the shoulders. She wore an apron and smelled of lemon dish soap. Her thinning hair seemed grayer than before. The lines around her eyes and mouth appeared etched deeper. Though she smiled up at him, there was a look of sadness in her green eyes.

"*Mutter*, I'm happy to see you." He carefully brought his booted left foot over the threshold.

"Richard, are you hurt?"

"It's nothing. Some stitches."

"Come...come...close the door. It is so cold outside."

The warmth of the home and the smell of cooking food enveloped him. He handed her his coat and surveyed the living room.

"No Christmas decorations?"

She hung his coat in the closet. "There is nothing to celebrate this year." Hands clasped together, she stood and looked at him. "Are you hungry?"

"I can wait until supper time. What room do you want me to stay in?"

"The guest room, if that's okay?"

"Oh, yes. That's perfect. Let me drop my stuff off." He took his bag upstairs and down the narrow hallway. There were pictures all over the walls. He dare not look knowing a picture of Gisele would stab him deep into his heart. The room was dark but tidy and the same as when he stayed during Gisele's funeral. He realized the last time he was in this room, he had plotted his revenge. Parting the curtains, he looked out the frosted windows at a frozen Lake Michigan stretching across the steel gray horizon.

Down in the kitchen, his mother-in-law was bustling between the stove, the sink and the counter. An old plastic radio set to WNWI played German American music. She didn't notice him right off and he watched her lost in cooking.

"Oh, Richard, would you like a Coke, coffee or tea?"

"No, I'm fine. Thanks." He pulled out a wire-backed chair from the round table in the breakfast nook. "What're you cooking? Smells good."

"*Schnitzel und Spatzle.* You always liked it."

"Yes. I do."

She drained noodles in the sink. "Was your drive okay?" She spoke quickly to cover a moment of silence.

"Yes. I missed the snow."

"There's so much snow this year."

"Yes. There is."

And they came upon another moment of silence.

She put the noodles and other ingredients into a pan and opened the oven. "Maybe...maybe tomorrow we can go and see Gisele?"

"I'd like that," he replied, not wanting to disappoint her by saying he had already been.

They stayed on superficial topics, with brief responses throughout dinner. Neither wanted to be the one to say something to upset the other.

Rich picked at his meal.

"Eat. Eat," his mother-in-law urged.

"It's difficult."

"Does it taste bad?"

"Not your cooking. I have no appetite. It all tastes bitter on my tongue."

Her voice caught. She managed to say, "I understand."

Rich cleared away the dishes from the table and started the water in the sink.

"No. No, Richard. I do the dishes."

"*Mutter*, I want to. Okay?"

They went into the living room. Rich appreciated that Frau Esslin kept the light low. A single Tiffany lamp on a table at the front window provided a half-lit glow. It wasn't that he liked the dark, he feared the pictures and memories along the mantle. The portraits on the walls, and all the knickknacks and curios of Gisele growing up hurt him to see.

His mother-in-law poured herself an Underberg from a side table and handed him a stem glass of white wine. Rich knew there was no avoiding it now; they would talk. Frau Esslin turned on the gas fireplace and dancing blue flames embraced ceramic logs. They sat on wing chairs facing the fire. She sipped, while Rich toyed with the wineglass and brooded on the flames.

"Do you sometimes see her walk in the room. You look up and she's gone?"

The yellow-tipped blue flames of the fire hissed.

"Do you want to see the letter from the attorney?"

"No, I can deal with all that tomorrow."

"Gisele has a large safe with files and important papers."

"Also tomorrow."

"How is your bar? Is it okay?"

"Yes. It is. I have some really good people working for me." He glanced over at her. "And you, *Mutter*? How are you doing?"

"It is very...trying."

"We set things up to take care of you after Willy's heart attack. You shouldn't have any worries. The house is paid for. There is a trust account that pays taxes and monthly bills."

"*Villy* left me five years ago. Gisele, you and Rudi were close by. But now Gisele is taken. I feel I am in a boat, on the ocean, alone."

"You're not. I can be here within hours. Perhaps Rudi should come home and live with you."

"Oh, I don't know." She brought the narrow digestif glass to her lips.

"I am sure Gisele made certain you were taken care of. We will see that tomorrow in her papers."

"Are the police looking for the men that killed Gisele?"

"Yes. I met with them last week. They have a pretty good idea who and are actively pursuing them." He thought it best to be circumspect.

"Good." She nodded and nodded, then fixed Rich with piercing eyes. "And your trip to India?"

"My trip?"

"This is where you hurt your foot?"

"An accident."

"Richard...did you find them?"

He didn't want to answer. But murmured, "Um-hm."

"Did you kill these men?"

Rich had vowed never to speak of it. Yet, the plea in her eyes made him glance down to the wineglass. Firelight gave the glass and wine an amber glow. His eyes lifted to meet hers.

"Did they suffer?"

Light and shadow played on the ceiling above.

"Yes."

She returned to the fire, light flickering across her face. Rich noted Frau Esslin's tight-lipped smile. "*Brenn in der Holle*," she whispered.

A long silence, broken by Rich setting his wineglass on the side table. "*Mutter*, it was a long drive today. I'm tired." He stood, then leaned over and kissed his mother-in-law on the top of her head.

Her plaintive eyes gazed up at him. "Thank you for coming to see this lonely old woman."

"I am here for you, *Mutter*."

"Good night."

"Good night." Rich paused at the foot of the staircase. "Is your wi-fi hooked up?"

"Oh, heavens, I left it on."

"I'll take care of it." He started up the stairs.

"If you're cold, there's a quilt in the linen closet."

"I know."

Rich quietly closed the guest room door and drew the curtains. Wind outside made the house creak, yet it remained snug and warm. He unstrapped the Velcro stays of the surgical boot and settled on the bed. The bottom of his foot itched. Gently he rubbed it. Snapping on the bedside light, he took out his laptop and leafed through his notes.

Sorting through the folders on his laptop, he opened a document entitled Money Laundering. The document on Nudelman read:

Boyko Nudelman, Russian/Jewish. Real estate broker, U.S. known associate Leonid "Tarzan" Fainberg.

"That's the link," he murmured.

Nudelman gained wealth during privatization after the collapse of the Soviet Union in the 1990s. He parlayed a tenement block in Kapotnya, a poor section of Moscow, into sizable real estate holdings. His tactic was to borrow on one building and put money down on two more buildings. Buildings were usually dilapidated former government-run housing. Worked like a Ponzi Scheme.

Nudelman helped finance Yeltzin's re-election.

Had an in with *Semibanckirshina*, the Seven Bankers.

Called a Kleptocrat for stashing money in Swiss bank accounts.

Convicted of bribing housing officials and inspectors to pass unsafe buildings.

Targeted for a purge by the Kremlin for less than enthusiastic support of the Putin regime.

Tax evasion charges made him flee Russian Federation for Tel Aviv.

Frozen out of Tel Aviv real estate, Nudelman ventured into drugs and human trafficking through Feinberg and his connection with the Franko Family and Cozmos Corporation. Suspected of being the money behind the purchase of a decommissioned Soviet Navy diesel submarine, which Feinberg tried to sell to a Columbian cartel to smuggle drugs into the United States.

Left Tel Aviv for "The Big Store" due to legal and money pressure.

Whereabouts: Sunny Isles, Florida. San Diego, California.

Medical note: has severe heart issues.

Rich opened his browser and typed in Boyko Nudelman Real Estate. Pages of results popped up.

A page for Nudelman Luxury Estates topped the list. Rich clicked on the site.

Bob Nudelman's Luxury California Estates filled the screen.

"Bob?"

To the right, at the top, was a large photo that appeared photoshopped, featuring a grinning Slavic man in suit and tie. Under the photo, the caption read: Robert 'Bob' Nudelman, Broker/Owner. He was posed, head at a slight angle. He had a large, broad forehead, pointy chin, flat cheeks and eyes slightly more narrow than Europeans. The smile was toothy and friendly for one with such bad teeth. But it was the eyes, mean slits that betrayed pure evil.

A double row of houses for sale in little boxes filled the rest of the web page. Luxury properties for sure. There were coastal cliffside properties in San Diego and smaller, but no less expensive, properties in hip Ocean City. No single listing was under one million dollars.

Rich clicked through links on the site, looking under management. And he found him. A small photo of Symon Roitman. His title—Office Manager. He leaned close and noted the cleft lip must've been photoshop erased.

"Gotcha."

He noted the San Diego address for Nudelman Real Estate and the contact email address. He clicked out of the web site and shut down his laptop. Laying in the quiet of the room he started to work it out.

Up before the dawn, Rich crept down to the kitchen. Yawning, he had not slept well, tossing and turning over how to get to Symon Roitman, the third man. He made coffee and dialed FBI agent Paul Bertoloni.

"You have reached Special Agent Paul Bertoloni. Please leave a message."

"Paul, this is Rich Rice. I am in Glencoe and would like to meet at your office. Call me back with a good time." He clicked off and reached for the coffee pot.

"I smelled coffee."

"Mornin' *Mutter*," Rich said. "I made a pot."

His mother-in-law, dressed in a thick velour brown robe, sleepy-eyed, shuffled slippers across the kitchen tile. She took down a decorative cup from a cabinet. "I make you breakfast."

"I usually just have toast," he said, sitting at the small round table.

"I make it." From habit, she switched on the radio to Om Pah Pah music.

Rich's phone beeped, indicating an incoming text. He opened the app.

"Don't call. Don't email. Don't text. Don't come here," the text read. It wasn't signed, and the number displayed only zeros. But Rich assumed it was from Bertoloni.

He read the text again. What was this all about?

Frau Esslin must've read the confused expression on his face. "Everything all right?"

"A weird text."

She brought over toast with one square pat of butter in the center of each browned slice. "From who?"

"Doesn't really matter. I just didn't understand the message."

"Write them back."

Rich put his phone face down on the table and picked up a piece of toast and knife. "Maybe later," he said, spreading the butter.

After breakfast, Rich drove his mother-in-law to the Skokie cemetery. They rode in silence, stopping once in town so Frau Esslin could buy flowers for Gisele's grave. Crunching a fresh layer of new snow, Rich's mother-in-law, flowers in her gloved hands, led the way down row upon row of gray monuments. She knelt at the marker and bowed her head, mumbling in German. Rich forgot his own grief and thought how devastating it must be for her to lose her daughter.

In a distant corner, a dirty yellow and black CAT backhoe belched black diesel smoke and chugged, its distended arm gouging out another hole.

"Someone has stolen her flowers," his mother-in-law said.

Rich stood at the foot of Gisele's grave, fists deep in his pockets, hiding the dead flowers. His thoughts turned to find the third man Roitmann and make him pay for taking Gisele.

"Do you need to stop anywhere?" he asked, glancing over, as they drove back.

"No," she replied, staring out the side window.

They were both lost in their own emotions.

When they returned, Rich hung up his mother-in-law's coat and his own, then went to the kitchen for coffee.

"I show you letter now."

Coffee in hand, Rich followed Frau Esslin up the stairs, down the hall to a room with a closed door. She opened the door to a dark, stuffy, close room.

Rich hesitated at the threshold. His mother-in-law went in and opened the curtains on a bay window. A large desk in the bay window had three computer monitors and upright files, with papers in stacked trays. This was Gisele's office.

In contrast, across the room was a day bed with flower quilt, bookcases displaying pictures of horses and young girls at summer camp. It took Rich aback.

His mother-in-law handed a letter off the desk and to Rich. "This is the letter from the lawyer." She opened the bi-fold door to the closet. "And in here are her files."

Rich sat on the squeaking day bed, reading.

The letterhead was from Cermak, Cicero & McCormack, venerable Chicago surnames, with offices in Winnetka and The Loop. Rich glanced down and the signature was Helmy E. Touhy. He didn't have any capital letters after his name, nor indication he was even a partner.

Rich murmured while scanning through the letter. "Estate of Gisele E. Rice...regarding brokerage accounts...release immediately to my clients...bring suit...liable for loss of earnings or dividends..." What a bunch of bullshit, thought Rich.

He pulled out the chair at Gisele's desk and turned on the computer tower. A blue screen came up with Ctrl-Alt-Del to open. A field in the middle needed a password.

"Shit."

"*Vas* is *das*?"

"I need Gisele's password." He rummaged through the desk drawer and found an old yellow sticky. In Gisele's block handwriting was written: Gis E R, and below that Lahaina92. Rich remembered they honeymooned in Lahaina in 1992. He typed in the log-in and password.

All three large monitors flickered on. The middle and monitor to the right had the market reports, colored lines and graphs, with a crawler at the bottom showing updated stock quotes. The monitor to the left displayed Bloomberg News. The setup mesmerized Rich a moment. "Babe, you had it so together."

"What was that Richard?" his mother-in-law asked.

"Nothing. Listen, this letter isn't anything to worry about. It's a bluff." Rich reached for a cell phone on the desk. He dialed the number of the law office.

"You have reached Cermak, Cicero and McCormack, attorneys at law," a recorded voice said. "No one is available to answer your call. Please leave a message with your name and number and an attorney will return your call." There was a beep.

"This is Richard Rice. I am responding to a letter sent to my late wife Gisele Rice from Helmy E. Touhy regarding her brokerage accounts. Call me at..." Rich looked at the handheld phone for the number. He added the number to the message and hung up.

Frau Esslin self-consciously shifted her stance, turned a framed portrait of her daughter slightly to the right, and swiped dust off a shelf. "I am going downstairs," she said.

Rich hardly noticed, saying, "Uh-huh," as he clicked on computer files.

She fled the room for the kitchen where warm coffee and German music comforted her.

He searched through the files and located documents authorizing Gisele to represent the accounts and make trades and stock sales in the name of the account holder.

The cell phone buzzed.

"This is Richard Rice."

"Mr. Rice, this is Helmy Touhy. I am responding to your phone call…"

"And I am responding to your threatening letter," Rich interrupted.

"Well, you needn't…" Touhy had a noticeably young sounding voice.

"I needn't what?"

"Take that tone."

"I'll take any tone I like. You threatened me with a lawsuit."

"Well…ah, we needed some action to resolve the matter."

"And why would you think I wouldn't resolve the matter?"

"We hadn't heard from you in weeks."

"Weeks? My wife was killed a month ago."

"And I am very sorry about that."

"Oh, are you now."

"Yes." Touhy breathed an audible sigh. "Listen. We've gotten off on the wrong foot."

"Not me."

"No, not you. And I apologize."

"I am executor of the estate, I have the POA and the death certificate. Copies will be priority mailed to the SEC and the accounts will be released to your clients."

"That's all we wanted."

"Anyone ever tell you your name sounds like spit."

"Excuse me?"

"Touhy," Rich emphasized the sound. "Touhy, like you're spitting into the gutter."

"There's no need for that."

"There was no need for your threats."

"We needed to get things done."

"Maybe. Touhy."

"All right—enough."

"The paperwork will get in and your clients will get their accounts returned to them within a week. I will get letters out to them and they will need to send certified letters with the name of the brokerage for the transfer."

"Thank you."

"You're welcome...*Touhy*," and Rich clicked off.

He pawed through files in Gisele's safe. She had a file with a life insurance policy worth two hundred and fifty thousand dollars. Rich looked through the document. Rudi and Frau Esslin split one hundred thousand, while Rich received one hundred and fifty thousand.

"Dammit," he whispered. "I don't want the money. I want you."

Rich clicked through computer files and found stocks and an IRA account in both their names. It was over a hundred thousand dollars.

"Shit," he murmured, almost angry.

Gisele's half interest in The Ordinary automatically went over to Rich. Something clattered in the bottom of the safe. Rich raised papers and saw a pile of silver dollars.

He started breaking down and packing up the computer tower and monitors.

Frau Esslin was at the door. "Are you leaving, Richard?"

"I think I should get back." He paused. "Gisele had an insurance policy with you as a beneficiary."

"She took such good care of me." At that moment, Frau Esslin sounded frail and vulnerable.

"And I will take good care of you as well. You will never want for money, nor a place to live, or anything. Okay?"

"Yes, thank you, Richard."

Rich continued boxing the computer. "Maybe you can go back to Germany and visit your sister."

"I will think about it. Right now, getting out of bed is difficult."

"I know what you mean." He wound a black cord into small loops. "She would've wanted us to go on."

"I know that."

"Was there anything for Rudi?"

"Yes. I will notify him and get him a check."

"You're a good man, Richard."

"Not good enough to save my wife's life."

A long slow drive back to Omaha on cruise control and in the right lane. Snow blew across the interstate but did not pile up. He had a lot to figure out. He drove toward the west with the sky a steel gray. There might be snow for Christmas.

"Anything exciting happen?" he asked Daisy as he came in from the kitchen.

"Nah," she replied. "Customers have started to thin out because of the weather and the holidays."

"Figured that would happen." Rich leaned over the bar. "Can I get a coffee, Riku?"

"A dash with a splash."

"That's the one." He turned back to Daisy. "You wanted to do something for Christmas?"

"Nothing big."

"I'd like us to get together and make sandwiches and food and take it down to the mission."

"Sounds good."

"And for New Year's, we can do a Big Beat night."

"Big Beat? What's that?"

"Sixties, and some soul." Rich sipped his coffee. "We'll get a DJ round."

"Oh, I just remembered. Hey Riku, pull out those letters for the Boss."

Riku handed over a pair of priority letters from under the bar.

Rich tapped the white envelopes on the bar. "I'll look at these later. I'm upstairs if you need me."

The wind had picked up. It bit on his back and nipped at his bare head as he carted boxes up the outside stairs to his second-floor flat.

CHAPTER 6

Rich's cell phone buzzed. It was Daisy, downstairs in the bar. She sounded almost frantic.

"Boss, there's a suit down here, standing in the middle of the bar. He's freaking everybody out," she hurriedly said. "He's got a barbershop haircut and looks like a cop, but maybe more than a cop."

"Check his shoes. If they are cheap, black and polished, he's trouble."

Rich heard Daisy off the phone. "Let me see your shoes."

"My what?"

"Your shoes."

It was quiet a moment.

"Black and polished."

Rich got up and took his Glock from the gun safe. "What's he want?"

"He won't say."

"I'll be right down."

"No. He says he knows you live upstairs. He wants to come up."

Rich's mind raced through the possibilities. A U.S. Marshall with extradition warrant? He'd have the advantage if he caught him on the stairs. "Okay. Lead him through the kitchen."

At the backdoor, Rich smacked in a magazine and clicked off the safety. He heard the kitchen door clatter, being unlocked. He slowly and quietly turned the knob and left the back door ajar. Voices softly exchanged: "He's up the stairs."

"Okay. Thanks." Footsteps resounded on the iron steps.

Rich waited.

The pulse of his heartbeat pounded in his ears, matching the mounting of the stairs.

He took a long breath and let it out slowly, evenly. He threw back the door and slipped out to the landing. The Glock concealed but obvious behind his back.

"Who are you?"

His face was fleshy, young and red from the winter wind. He looked up in surprise. "I'm..I'm..."

"You're who?"

"I mean, I was sent by Agent Bertoloni with a message."

"Stop right there. Give it here."

He reached up with a folded page.

Rich read by the orange light over the landing. *Meet me at Saturday, five. Wear a suit jacket.* The address was in Dundee, on Farnum between 50th and 52nd streets.

"You got anything more for me?"

"Well...no."

"Then get the hell off my property."

The young agent went slowly down the stairs.

"Now!" Rich yelled.

The agent took off running out of the parking lot.

He read the note over and over as he went back into his flat. Why a suit jacket? All he had was a black or gray jacket. Those were his choices. It dawned on him that this must be the rehearsal dinner hosted by the groom's family.

Sitting at the table, he absentmindedly opened other priority letters and pulled out the papers. Rich sat up in his chair.

There was a partially completed birth certificate for the Republic of Panama. Rich read through: missing were a name, father's name, city of birth—but there was an embossed seal of the Republic and a signature from the head of Passport Authority, Panama.

A sticky note held by a paper clip showed Borodavka's poor handwriting: finish this, scan and print out, attach an old passport photo. Include two pre-paid credit cards for ten thousand USD each and send by priority mail to the address provided.

He wondered why Borodavka was taking the chance of putting his name on this.

Rich clicked on his scanner and filled in a name— Richardo de la Guarda. He matched the type with American Typewriter. Perfect? No, but the border guards would be looking at the passport photo and not the birth certificate.

Being a journalist, these days meant you knew a little bit about a lot—but less than you used to know. Rich lost himself matching typefaces and trying to replicate the birth certificate. He didn't need to count headlines or adjust lead-ing or the kerning. As for measuring the space in picas—who knew what a pica was anymore?

Those memories of going to the back shop because they were shorthanded or one of the girls in composing had a sick cat, Rich relished.

Stripping in liner corrections, pasting up mechani-cals or long rows of classified was hard work way back when. Every morning the publisher would drop a copy of the news-paper on each desk in news, sports, editorial and ads and say: "There it is...the Daily Miracle."

He got the birth certificate done, complete with a jumper on the letter "m." Tomorrow he'd get pictures then to the bank and load the credit cards. Either he'd been taken for twenty thousand dollars, or he'd receive a blue-jacketed passport from the Republic of Panama.

"Black or gray?"

The last time Rich wore his black suit was at Gisele's funeral, so gray it would be.

Under a canopy of old-growth maple and other trees, Dundee, originally a suburb of Omaha, was an older neigh-borhood now in Midtown Omaha, older by about 140 years and very well-heeled. Rich searched for numbers on the Co-lonials, Georgians and Tudor Revivals. He checked the curb-ing.

The cars filling any available parking space in and around a house with couples dressed in suits and fancy dress gave away the location. Rich went round and round the block, looking for enough curb to park his truck. He found a spot on the other side of the block.

The house was a Tudor Revival with a steep roof, narrow casement windows on the second floor and gables. Its half-timber exterior with picturesque chimney and storybook entry was fronted by an immaculate short sloping lawn with hedges by the house, sides and sidewalk.

A beefy, ex-football player type in a suit stopped Rich with a big meaty hand on his chest. He had a microphone clipped to his lapel.

"You on da list?"

"List?"

"Guest list."

"Oh," Rich pulled the invitation from his inside pocket and handed it to the security guy.

The air was cold and crisp and Rich bunched his suit coat around him.

"Dere's no name on dis."

"That's what they gave me." Rich shrugged. "This is the Bertoloni house, isn't it?"

"Who?"

"FBI Agent Paul Bertoloni."

"Bertoloni? Dis is the Nutkis house, Federal Prosecutor Nutkis."

"Ohhhhhh."

"Stay put." The security guard half-turned and talked low into his lapel. Within a minute, another security guard came up and whispered in the guard's ear. "Okay...you awright. Go on in." He made a checkmark on the invite and handed it back to Rich.

The entryway was crowded with couples in clumps of four or five, talking and drinking, Rich sidestepped the crush and entered the larger living room. An ornate stained wood and brick fireplace in a corner held a roaring, crackling fire that radiated warmth throughout the room. Short-coated waiters and waitresses roved about with trays of fluted glasses.

A string quartet could be heard in a distant room.

"Excuse me," Rich said, pausing a waiter long enough to pluck a glass. He held the glass to the light. It had a deep golden hue.

"French, sir," the waiter murmured, disappearing.

Rich took a sip. No alcohol bite. It had ultrafine bubbles from the second fermentation and a honey taste that lingered on the tongue.

Across the room, bald and standing head and shoulders above the older couple he seemed to be sharing a joke with was Nutkis. He wore a gray tweed blazer with open collar white shirt. The brown slacks spoiled the look He spotted Rich and straightened up. He could not suppress his displeased expression while weaving his way over.

Nutkis led with his open hand. "Not often, in fact never, have I welcomed to my home a person who I tried my damnedest to indict for murder."

Rich shook his hand. "Well, doctors bury their mistakes; prosecuting attorneys serve them French Champagne."

"Indeed."

"Let's not relitigate. Congratulation on your daughter's marriage."

"That's not until tomorrow. I still have time to talk her out of it. But, thank you, Mr. Rice."

"Rich."

"All right, Rich." A waiter stopped and let Nutkis take his time selecting a flute.

Rich exchanged an empty for a full flute.

"To Freedom," Nutkis saluted Rich.

Rich acknowledged the gesture. "Or marriage."

Nutkis vented a breathy laugh.

"I'm joking."

"I know."

"I run a bar in South Omaha and I have to say this champagne is several grades better than the best I have hidden in the basement."

"Moet & Chandon. Sometimes plea bargains in an ATF case can reap untoward rewards." Nutkis drained the champagne. "I have heard your little bar is oddly named but serves top quality food."

"Thanks. Come by some time and I'll stake you and your wife to a meal."

"I'm a widower," Nutkis replied, giving Rich a penetrating look. "Which reminds me...my deepest sympathies to you on the loss of your wife."

"Ahhhh," awkward and not sure how to respond, Rich muttered, "thanks. And my condolences..."

"No need. That was five years ago," Nutkis waved the comment away. He changed the subject. "I'll let Paul know you are here. And our ubiquitous amigo Borodavka is somewhere in this mix."

"Hide the enchiladas," Rich smiled, sipping, relieved.

"I need to circulate, you understand. Sorry for trying to send you up the river."

"No need to apologize. Sorry for beating you."

Nutkis laughed and paused before slipping into the crowd. "It was the dog, you know."

"My dog? Roommate?"

"When you told the jurors Nickolai Franko killed your dog, I knew I was sunk. No jury is going to indict a man for killing the guy that killed his dog."

"I'd rather my dog lived." That was the truth.

Nutkis waved.

Rich slowly took a tour through the house. In a room off the kitchen, he noticed Borodavka with a small, mousy woman in the act of berating the large lawyer. Must be Mrs. Borodavka, Rich thought.

He sauntered through the kitchen with its gleaming stainless-steel appliances. He took a potato chip from a large bowl and dipped it in ranch sauce. Quality champagne and American oily, salty snacks. The table was laid out in the usual chips & salsa or bean dip; vegetable tray and a cup of tan dip that was untouched. Oh, Rich realized, hummus untouched.

French doors off the kitchen opened on a large tent out back with long tables dressed in white linen and a china service. Heaters were placed here and there.

The string quartet played in the middle of the tent, shivering through Bach's *Jesu Joy of Man's Desiring*.

Molly Nutkis stood in the center of a gaggle of giggling girls that must've been her bridesmaids. She saw Rich at the same moment and offered a sly smile and wink. He beat a hasty retreat.

People he did not know nodded greetings. He politely acknowledged them. They were buttoned-down and too conservative to be sitting along the bar at The Ordinary.

In the living room, he found a corner space and traded his empty flute for a fresh one.

Bending over talking to an older, wispy gray-haired couple was Bertoloni in a full black suit, with a gray tie. He caught sight of Rich. The couple must've been his parents and they appeared overwhelmed by it all.

Smiling and slapping a back or two, Bertoloni traversed the room as if it were an obstacle course.

"You might've shaved," Bertoloni said.

"Growing it out."

Bertoloni reached to touch Rich's scruffy beard. It was a dominance move and Rich brought his left elbow up, fending off Bertoloni's hand. As he did, he punched the FBI agent in his chest with the heel of his right hand.

Bertoloni staggered back.

Four or five people around the room made a move toward them.

"I knew it."

"Can't be too careful."

"I thought this was your house."

"Oh, God, no. We're old-line Italians from the east side of 13th Street."

"Why didn't you text me back?"

"We can't talk here. Come on."

Bertoloni slid back a pocket door to a den.

They startled two guests in a clinch.

The woman hastily buttoned and brushed down her blouse. The man wiped his mouth on a handkerchief.

"Agents. I suggest you take that elsewhere."

"Sir." They scrambled out.

Definitely a masculine room and well-appointed with polished wood and forest green walls and green plaid carpet. Bookcases of law books and textbooks, with some novels, lined one wall, divided by a drinks cabinet and over-stuffed brown leather chair. A clawfoot mahogany desk sat opposite a latticed window. It must've been Nutkis' library

There were commendation photos on the walls, a collection of "grab and grin" photos and many family photos of Nutkis, his wife and two sons and Molly, his daughter, and Bertoloni's bride.

The FBI agent helped himself to cigars from a round humidor on the desk. He then went over and closed the pocket door. Rich eyed him reproachfully.

"You, my friend, are hot stuff." He offered a cigar.

Rich declined. "Hot stuff?"

"Saturday night stolen car hot."

"Why?"

"There's an Interpol Red Notice for your extradition to India with backing from our State Department."

"Don't know what you're talking about." Rich went to the front window, fidgeting with his champagne glass.

"Sure you don't...like the four charred bodies you left be-hind in Northern India." Bertoloni paused. "I can't help you, or talk to you, or even be seen with you."

"That why you didn't respond to my text?"

"Pretty much.

"Worried about your career?"

"Partly," Bertoloni replied, turning the cigar end round and round under the wooden match. "Not wanting U.S.

Marshalls turning up in my office asking inconvenient questions about your whereabouts. I can't lie."

"Don't blame you for that." Rich regarded Bertoloni a moment.

"Why would India care to extradite an American for allegedly killing Russian Mafia?"

"They don't...India, I mean. No doubt it's their ally, neighbors to the north putting pressure on them. The Bear wants you bad...and close enough to grab."

Rich could hear the crackle of Bertoloni puffing on the cigar. He spewed smoke; it was sweet and oppressive. "You know what will happen to you if they extradite you to India?"

"I have a pretty good idea."

"The average time people are held prior to trial is five years. You, being a foreigner, would not get anything close to resembling bail. You'd be five years sitting in an overcrowded, unsanitary communal prison like Tihar Jail Number 4, Tihar Village, Delhi."

"I have the law on my side."

"How do you think that?" Bertoloni half-laughed.

"Punishment for murder is death or life imprisonment. They are pretty strict. A conviction is difficult without an undisputed eyewitness or confession."

"Were there witnesses?"

"I think not."

They were quiet a moment, Bertoloni smoking. Rich stared out the front window.

"Maybe I'll take up with the Naxals or the Maoists. The Naxals march under red and yellow umbrellas, with a hammer and sickle."

"Naxals? Maoists? What in the name of Stinky Magoo is that?"

"Naxals are a communist group out of West Bengal. They can be particularly violent, although they seem to cohabitate peacefully with the crazy quilt of fringe political groups throughout the subcontinent."

"I'd still advise you to surrender to the U.S. Marshals. State might give you a hearing and determine India doesn't have enough compelling evidence for them to turn you over."

"Let me worry about that." Rich paused. "If you are so worried about being seen with me, how is it you can talk to me now?"

"Accident. You were invited long ago." Bertoloni took a long draw. "Like it or not, we're tangled up together."

"So, my ass is your career."

"In a word...solid."

"You know what it is I want to know."

"I do." Bertoloni puffed great blue clouds. "Omaha Metro brought me up to speed on your meeting." The agent took a deep drag. "You are on the right track with Boyko Nudelman and Symon Roitmann."

"Okay." Rich stared over his shoulder. "What do you know about Nudelman?"

"Nothing you don't already know." Bertoloni let his head fall back and blew smoke to the ceiling.

"His heart disease?"

Rich's eyes bored into the tall man. The FBI agent studied the glowing end of the cigar.

Bertoloni looked surprised. "Heart disease? It's bad...very bad. He's not allowed stimulants and is on Nitro, I think."

"That helps me."

"I have said too much. Honesto Ogg might want to get you up-to-speed on this."

"The midget."

"Hey."

"Hey what?"

"Ogg will keep an eye on what you're up to—especially if you're on the wrong track. What have you got in mind?"

"Nothing."

"Sure. I believe that. Don't do anything stupid." Bertoloni stuffed a couple more cigars in his inside pocket, starting for the door. "I'm teaching a three-part seminar called The Coming Clash."

"My favorite band."

"The clash between MS-13 in the West and the Eastern European Mafia in the East."

"Sounds familiar." Rich finished his champagne.

"I quote your news articles," Bertoloni said. "And I give you credit."

"Oh, thanks very much."

"Don't be like that."

"You're right." Rich had to agree. "How is Lieutenant Lavender? Any progress?"

Bertoloni's head dropped a moment. "He didn't make it. He died last night from the wounds he received in the gunfight at The Ordinary."

"Damn," Rich breathed.

CHAPTER 7

No snow on Christmas, but bitter winds and a biting cold gripped the Missouri Valley. A cold that sliced through wool, fleece and any other layer.

The interstate was icy and dangerous and Rich declined going to his mother-in-law's for Christmas.

The nights were lonely.

The weather kept people away from The Ordinary. Regulars would show, but the crowds thinned out due to the holidays, the weather, etc.

Rich gave each of The Ordinary employees, Daisy, Riku, the twins and Jorge a five-hundred-dollar bonus for the year. Jorge held the check in his hand, his face contorted, almost succumbing to tears. "I not ever get a bonus in any job. I thank you, *Jefe*."

"Buy your *tres angels* something special for Christmas."

The certified letters had gone out to all of Gisele's clients and accounts moved to other brokerage houses. Rich parked the account Gisele had set up with them with one of those custodian types that just administered the account, but wasn't aggressive with investments.

The Christmas party was a small affair, but fun. The people that came were the regulars. Rich's Big Beat New Year's Eve had a better crowd, with a DJ spinning 45s of mid-sixties music.

He waited for the priority letter from Panama Passport Authority. After three weeks, he had all but given up the ten grand for lost when an envelope came. It contained a blue jacketed Panamanian passport, a birth certificate and a temporary driver's license.

Meanwhile, he continued to research Nudelman's real estate business, determining it was a money-laundering operation, selling homes at prices over asking and reselling at lower prices. The difference was clean, untraceable money.

Rich turned the keyboard to his hands and opened his email account.

Mr. Nudelman,

My name is Richardo de la Guarda and I am a successful Panamanian businessman.

He stopped and deleted the line.

I am a highly successful Panamanian businessman. I have found myself with a surplus of money and need to invest in real estate to avoid taxes.

I will be in San Diego next week and would like to meet with you regarding buying some prime real estate properties.

>*Sincerely,*
>*Richardo de la Guarda*

He clicked on send.

Doodling on a legal-size yellow pad Rich filtered through ideas and took some notes.

Drive to Nogales. Too long a drive. He crossed it off the pad.

Drive from Omaha to Phoenix—he keyed in the query—20-hour drive and change—total of 1365 miles--highway 25 south, and highway 40. That was do-able, more so than Nogales.

He'd put his truck in long-term parking at the Phoenix airport, then stay the night at an airport hotel under Richardo de la Guarda. He needed to establish de la Guarda's presence in the U.S.

The morning, as Richardo, he would fly from Phoenix to Las Vegas.

Searching, he found a two-star, off-the-strip "resort" in Las Vegas—the Immigrant Isle Hotel and Casino and made a reservation. He'd reserve five nights in Las Vegas, rent a car the following morning and drive to San Diego.

Once in San Diego, he had to play up the part of a rich Panamanian businessman, so he'd book the airport Hilton and contact Nudelman.

From that point on, he couldn't plot what might happen. He'd have to read the situation and react, acting out the scene. It got to him, fear wriggling up his spine, wondering if he'd be able to pull it off.

There were some chores he needed to take care of prior. Banking on the diagnosis that Nudelman's heart disease was advanced, Rich went to a sports nutrition store.

"Do you have caffeine or something to give me a boost in my workouts? I can put it in a shake before I work out...sort of kick me in the backside."

The buff young man, in a muscle t-shirt, behind the counter looked Rich over. "Not sure we stock that much."

"Funny." Rich did not laugh.

The man came out from behind the counter. "Follow me." He had a bow-legged, overly muscled walk and led Rich to a shelf of boxes, bottles and large round cans. He squatted.

Rich squatted alongside. His knees cracked.

"This is a caffeine-based product and available in a variety of strengths." He pulled a bottle of pills from the shelf. "These are moderate strength pills and will get you going. But you'll soon get a tolerance for them." He duck-walked down the aisle.

Rich was not going to try that. He stood and moved alongside the muscled youngster.

"These are our highest strength caffeine products. This powder you can add to a drink or something. He turned the can and squinted, reading the long list of ingredients. First on the list was caffeine. "I caution you to be really careful with this stuff. Start with a half a teaspoon or even a quarter—just to see what effect it has on you."

"Gotcha."

"A quarter teaspoon is about equal to a single cup of coffee."

"I might take that. Have you got anything stronger?"

"Stronger?" The young man eyed Rich. "Yeah."

"Ephedra. It's legal in this state. I'd be real careful with that stuff, though. It can be lethal, especially if you have any heart issues." He picked up a small can with a plain label.

"What is it?"

"It's from Ma Huang, an organic herb, Chinese, and can be really potent." The man shook his hand like he'd been burned. "Too much of this stuff and you're a goner."

"I'll take it."

"You sure?"

"Yup. Ring it up."

Nudelman would not, but Roitmann definitely knew what Rich looked like. It was the reason Rich grew his hair and hadn't shaved in weeks.

In India, he'd used makeup for his skin tone, and wore a tattered cassock to impersonate a beggar. There are so many poor in India, he just became another of a legion of sorry souls who lived on the dreadful side of good fortune.

It would be more difficult to disguise himself as a beggar in this country. And a Panamanian drug dealer would flaunt his money.

Rich dyed his unruly hair black, with white streaks at the temples. He did the same to his facial hair, with spots of white. He went to a stylist and got his beard trimmed and hair shaped.

Little changes worked best. He stuffed foam rubber between his left lower jaw and cheek, giving his face an asymmetry as if he'd had a stroke.

A set of clothes to match and Rich spent many days in men's clothing stores looking for a well-tailored (but not too well-tailored) suit. He found a brown suit, wide tie, and shoes to match the personality of the moneyed and well-heeled south of the border gentleman. He added a pair of tight, highly polished brown Oxfords. The shoes were too narrow across the toes. It altered Rich's stride.

Altogether, the suit and white dress shirt worked. But a couple of things were needed. And on the way out of the men's store, he saw it—a wide-brimmed fedora and pair of round, thick black frame clear lens glasses a la Leon Trotsky. Now he'd become Richardo, a rich Panamanian business-man of dubious dealings.

Richardo and Nudelman exchanged emails. Nudelman probed—how did Richardo get his money? What did he do? Rich gave as little information as he could, but enough to build his character profile.

The emails are an interrogation. He knew he'd get the same questions in San Diego. If the answers did not match, Rich would be in trouble.

"How is it I have not heard of you before?"

I'm careful.

"Any contacts I may know?"

Yes.

"Who told you about me?"

I was told you were a good contact.

"Who?"

Rich took some time to consider his response. He knew Nudelman was a former associate of Ukrainian Leonid Fain-berg, who was doing time in a Guatemala prison.

An inmate in Guatemala. He waited for a reply.

After a time, the email came in. "What do you want?"

To buy real estate.

"How much money do you have to buy or invest?"

Rich realized he was being vetted. He needed to consider his replies.

Enough.

"Call when you hit town."

A cautious, and careful, guy, thought Rich.

CHAPTER 8

Daisy stood stunned, her arms stiff at her sides, with little fists and visibly upset by Rich's new look. She knew, without him telling, he would be gone for a time. She became angrier when he refused to tell her where he would be.

"You're going to outsmart yourself, Boss," she said, teeth clenched, withholding her bite.

"Perhaps," he replied with a shrug, not disagreeing.

Rich took Jorge aside and asked if he knew any Panamanians.

Jorge gazed up at the ceiling, thinking a moment.

"I have cousin, she date Panama dude."

"What was he like?"

"Pozzy."

"Gay?"

"Oh, no." The cook's face screwed up like he'd smelled something turned. "He a man, but pozzy. Pozzy with clothes, food, on it you name."

"Do you mean prissy?"

"That what I say."

"He really got manners and no talk."

Rich looked at Jorge. "Quiet?"

"Not no talk, but no talk much. Couple words and he take long time to say."

Green dashboard lights lit the truck cab. Headlights bored through the pre-dawn darkness. Snow flurries chased Rich out of Omaha and stalked his drive down highway 25 south.

The radio played low, barely audible, sports talk, background noise.

Rich thought about his dog, Roommate. The Boston Terrier would be curled up on the passenger seat, half asleep but ready.

He missed that dog.

Gisele, his murdered wife, occupied most of his thoughts. He hurtled closer to his confrontation with the third man.

He would never have his wife back.

The further south he drove, the less snow accumulated. The highway asphalt turned wet and black.

Rich faced another eighteen hours on the road, at the wheel, in this 1300 and change-mile drive to Phoenix.

Daisy's silence and displeasure meant more than Rich had let on.

He mentally ticked off what he carried. The whole Richardo de la Guarda persona, from the Panamanian passport, fake driver's license, to clothing, credit cards and about ten thousand dollars in cash to flash and play up Richardo, the successful Panamanian criminal. Over and over he practiced his backstory. He was certain he'd have to recite the tale to Nudelman a couple times over.

Rich's worry lay in the planning. He had it down—up to a point—when he contacted Nudelman. He could not predict how the real estate broker would react, maybe. Rich had to think of possible scenarios Nudelman would throw in his direction trying to trip him up.

The Ukrainian had shown himself to be extremely wary, cautious and paranoid in the emails he and Rich had exchanged. Rich had to be ready on a variety of unknown levels.

Rich calculated Nudelman would want a contact, someone in Panama to call and find out who the rich Richardo de la Guarda was. It cost him another thousand dollars, but Borodavka had—reluctantly and not too happy about it— promised to have his Panamanian contact say *Richardo es Malo Hombre* if Nudelman called.

Borodavka said this stretched attorney/client privilege to near breaking point. He wanted no part, nor knowledge of anything else Rich cooked up.

An hour past dawn, Rich turned off at York and drove toward Hebron. A depressing little town. The highway for a couple of blocks was populated with fast food joints, gas stations and a couple of bars. Rich did not want to stop. The snow/rain had turned to drizzle.

The radio station out of Omaha started to broadcast static. The signal wavered in and out. He turned it off.

Cows, corn, cows, corn, cows, state trooper, corn, cows, corn, cows, and little else as the day and miles wore on. The highway unfolded a long way down the flatlands.

Kansas—Liberty, Freedom, Concordia—five hours.

Rich gassed up in Concordia and went in for coffee and a peanut butter cookie. Gisele's favorite cookie was peanut butter. The first bite and taste filling his mouth reminded him of her.

"Miss you, babe," he muttered, cookie in his mouth, wheeling the truck back onto the highway.

The cloudless, worn-out blue sky went on until it fell behind the edge of the world far down the road ahead.

He'd lunch in Salina, Kansas at the junction of 70 west.

A Kansas cowboy in a faded flannel shirt and beat straw hat, with coffee cup poised before his mouth, sat in the corner of the diner's dirty plate glass window. The diner stood on the far edge of Salina, a white-washed plywood building in need of a new roof. Rich sauntered in. The cowboy gave him a look, then glanced away. At the counter, he straddled a chrome and plastic covered stool. Rich ordered a hamburger. Greasy and wet, but tasty. The fries were limp and improved with ketchup.

At a corner table, an old man in a wheelchair stared off while a younger man fed him from a bowl. He wore old clothes and had a corner of a paper napkin tucked in the neckband of a dirty t-shirt. There were liver spots speckling his forehead and bald pate. His skin was white as birch bark. No brown spots, but the younger man bore a strong facial resemblance. He would hold a spoonful to the old man's mouth. He opened. The young man wiped the older man's mouth and chin.

Garfield, junction 156. Another town named Lincoln. Had to be a town named Lincoln in every state.

Rich and Gisele's mother stood at the big bay window, watching mourners climb into their cars at Gisele's funeral.

"Have coffee, Richard."

"With brandy would be nice."

Rich followed his mother-in-law into the kitchen. "Was she happy, *Mutter*?"

His mother-in-law looked up quickly, surprised. "Yes, very." Mrs. Esslin poured a jigger of brandy into his coffee cup.

"You're not just saying that." Rich took the offered coffee.

"You were her one." His mother-in-law paused. "*Mein Popi*, Villy, my husband, had doubts, but I could tell when you two were together."

"She...Gisele," his voice caught. "Was the smartest, most beautiful woman I have ever known. Not sure what she saw in a struggling journalist from northeastern Oregon."

"She saw a man who loved her and would support her. She saw what you would become."

Women, mature women, with short hair, seem to exude a certain kind of inner confidence.

A cascade of memories poured through Rich's thoughts as he drove on.

Seven and a half hours and Rich reached Oklahoma at the border, passing through Liberal, Kansas into the panhandle of Texas and Oklahoma. He wondered if any towns were named Liberal. There was a town of Republican and river of the same name in Nebraska. Crickets rocked on the high scrub hills among lazy longhorn cattle in the distance.

They'd married at the Glencoe, Illinois house and honeymooned in Maui. Those were sweet and wonderful days. They lay in the sun on the beach; chased each other down

Front Street; dined in town; and sat under the filtering sun-light of the Banyan tree.

Rich read the plaque in the park at the corner of Front and Canal streets. "This tree was planted in 1873."

"Old, isn't it," Gisele said with a snarky sideways grin.

They'd made love long into the night.

Highway 54 dived into Texas and north. Gas stations were few. Rich gassed up every chance he got.

Eleven hours on the road was wearing on him. He reached the northeast corner of New Mexico. Through Logan, New Mexico at Ute Lake Park. The sun lay low and started to wane—he had logged over 700 miles. Ready to call it a day, the highway linked up at Tucumcari. Billboards advertising the Dinosaur Museum started miles before town. All there was seemed to be was land, land and more land until New Kirk and Santa Rosa.

Rich pulled into the Motel Serengeti, promising cozy beds, free TV and phone on the marque.

"I'd like a room for the night."

"You're in luck; we have two left," the hotel clerk with a bleached blonde flip, said. She had a chubby face that seemed pinched together at the cheeks and mouth. She seemed quite young to have dedicated herself to accumulating so much girth. "That'll be sixty dollars."

Rich signed in with an unintelligible scrawl and used the Richardo de la Guarda credit card.

"Mr., um, Guardie," the clerk had her head twisted sideways trying to read. "Check out is at eleven in the morning. We offer a continental breakfast."

"How nice," Rich replied. "Can I get a key?"

A standard road motel room, neither chic, mostly shabby with mismatched coverlet, and general décor of ratty furniture. Dousing his face, Rich noticed the water had a smell, not iron, but the sharp aroma of rot. He slipped the chain on the door and fell backward into the bed. He sank in the middle. The definite biting stink of old sweat pervaded the room. His eyes burned. Before Rich closed his eyes, he noticed a wad of purple gum stuck to the popcorn ceiling above the bed.

Long trains rumbled through the night—every twenty minutes.

CHAPTER 9

Rich fought through heavy sleepiness, hitting the road at four something, or what he thought as four as Tumcuari was on Mountain time. Four something was actually three something. Tired, sore from eleven hours sitting yesterday, he was nevertheless buoyant to be back on the road headed west.

He bypassed Albuquerque and linked to highway 40. With snow-capped mountains in his rearview mirror, Rich realized he was on old Route 66. Thoreau, Gallup, then south on Highway 17 toward Flagstaff. Phoenix was clear sailing.

The rising sun at his back lit up reddish rock formations and barren scrub brush and sandy landscapes, with clusters of buildings and scattered subdivisions cropping up here and there and later down the road.

Radio scanned through stations that were mostly Spanish-speaking.

A surprising number of cars and trucks hurtled along the asphalt.

Bouncy, concertina music jumped to fast-talking sports and English-speaking religious programs. It all irritated him.

His breakfast of a day-old donut and cup of tepid coffee from a convenience store gas station did not satisfy.

The day heated up quickly. Still and dry and dusty air ached inside his lungs with each breath.

Billboards for hotels and restaurants heralded his approach to Phoenix—ninety-nine miles ahead.

From a yellowish haze, the city rose out of the flat desert floor ahead.

When in Phoenix visit...sixty-two miles away.

The sprawl of Phoenix started, and soon the skyscrapers, rising out of the desert floor stood in stark relief of the raw, reddish-brown upslope of the Superstition Mountains in the distance.

Rich followed the signage to Sky Harbor International Airport. He got into the lane for long-term parking and went around. He took a ticket at the entrance and put it in the glove compartment. There were parking spots way in the back. He passed on under a tree, the spot speckled with bird droppings.

He wheeled into a parking space and turned off the engine. The sudden quiet after hours on the road unsettled him.

"Okay. Here we go."

That early morning start got him to Sky Harbor by two in the afternoon.

The satchel bag held all the elements of Richardo de la Guarda. He changed-out wallets and made sure he had the brown suit, Oxford shoes, bolo string tie, glasses and other items of clothing. He checked the cologne he got for Richardo, the Panamanian dandy. Opening the small, stylized bottle, Rich took a whiff and winced. It smelled fruity yet flamboyant.

He put his burner phone in the glove compartment. Richardo would pick up one along the way.

Locking his truck, Rich hustled to the half shelter to catch the shuttle to the terminal.

"Southwest," he replied to the pear-shaped driver, who appeared to be part of the driver's seat, as he boarded the shuttle.

"Terminal four." The bifold door shut and the shuttle drove to the next pickup point.

The terminal seemed cavernous and it took Rich a minute to orient himself and locate the line at the Southwest counter.

"A ticket to Las Vegas."

"We have a flight in an hour," the short and stout agent said, adding, "One way? Or round trip?"

"One way." Richardo handed his passport and credit card over the counter.

"Any luggage to check, Mr. de la Guarda?"

"No."

The agent leafed to the back of Richardo's passport. "I don't see a stamp. How did you get into the United States?"

He screwed up. He immediately realized he should've gone through passport control.

"Is problem?"

"Yes and no. How did you enter the United States?"

"Nogales. I drive over at Nogales." His forehead was hot, his temples wet.

"And you drove all the way to Phoenix?" The agent thought it over. People were gathering behind Richardo. "Hmmm...I guess it's okay." He handed Richardo his passport and credit card. "Here's your boarding pass and documents. Go to Immigration entry and get stamped. I guarantee you won't get past TSA if you don't."

"Ahhh, *si. Gracias*. I mean thank you."

Think. Think, Rich chastised himself as he left the counter and went to the Immigration entry point. It took him a while to get to the head of the line.

"Purpose of your visit?" the tired-eyed agent asked in a monotone from behind thick plexiglass.

Richardo pushed his passport under the window. "Pleasure."

"Do you have," the agent perked up, "your airline ticket."

"I am going to Las Vegas."

"No, from your flight in." The agent's voice raised a few decibels like he was talking to a child. "How did you get in the United States?"

"I drive here."

"From where?"

"Panama City."

"Panama City? That's quite ah-ways. Can I see your driver's license?"

"It not far," Richardo said as he pulled the temporary U.S. license from his pocket. His temples were wet again.

"And where did you cross over?"

"Nogales."

"You must like to drive."

"*Si*, with *musica* it *tranquillo*...relax me."

"Apparently," the agent said slowly. "Everything seems in order, if not a tad bit odd." He stamped the passport and slipped them in the metal tray beneath the plexiglass.

"*Gracias*." And Richardo fast-walked through the congested terminal to the gate for his flight. He fell into his seat and audibly sighed, wiping the sweat from his face. You got to think...you got to anticipate, he growled to himself. Forget one little thing and it could be your life.

An aging propeller-driven puddle-jumper took forty-five minutes bouncing through the air before lining up its approach to McCarren International.

Walking from the gate to the rental car row, Rich spotted a mobile phone kiosk. A dot, not a feather, Indian fidgeted on a stool playing a game. Snapping his fingers, Rich got the man's attention and bought a phone.

Renting a large black SUV was a little more involved as Richardo was a foreign national, or "furiner" as the clerk called him. After a sheaf of paperwork, Rich took the shuttle connection to the rental car lot.

He waited a long time at the intersection, looking for a break in traffic. He accelerated into a hole in the flow and then found his way onto The Strip. Night had crept on, and the gaudy lights and neon flashing glowed against a serene desert dusk. Tourists crowded the walkways going down and going up The Strip. Everything seemed in motion, even the casinos and hotels.

Rich found East Flamingo and slowly eased through tourists ignoring the traffic signal.

If possible, the gaudiness of The Strip lost some of its luster by the casinos on East Flamingo. The tourists thinned out and the class petered out quickly. Rich made a mental note if he grew listless, the National Atomic Testing Museum was just down the street.

Once off The Strip, the glitz isn't that glamorous, the lights don't offer perpetual daylight, a neon tan, the tramp of tourists is less so, the fountains are few, the winners are far away, unclean air like desperation makes every breath a choke.

Wan, grimy tube lights, shaped like a palm tree on a deserted island, flashed left, flashed right, and racing lights circled a large sign proudly declaring: Black Jack, Craps, Poker, Slots, Sports Betting, Every Player Wins and fronted the entrance to Emigrant Isle, Casino and Resort. A drooping arrow on a Park Here sign directed Rich around to the back of the five-story, nondescript structure.

Rich bumped into the lot and found an open spot under a light.

He got hit by five card slappers walking up the block to the entrance. A skinny black youth had overturned a cardboard box and was dealing Three-Card Monty.

"How 'bout you, M'man. Find the red queen." His bony fingers stuffed and juggled the three cards. "Feelin' lucky, Cap'n? Pick the little lady and win."

What might've passed for a dressy vagrant or the Emigrant Isle doorman, lounged off to the side, finishing a smoke. Rich gave him a look and got a casual nod in return.

Pulling open the heavy glass and metal door, Richardo walked into noise and harsh light. To the left was the reception desk; to the right was The Treasure Room, the casino area. A fat-bellied guard wearing brown pants and a khaki shirt, armed with a 9mm automatic stood by the entrance to the Treasure Room.

Row upon row of chrome slot machines all but filled the expansive room. Bells, buzzers, dingers, beepers, lights and unrecognizable electronic noises made Rich think he could empty a .32 and none of the slot zombies would raise their eyes from the spinning tumblers. An old woman had coils of tickets festooned round her neck like beads the girl with the prettiest tits wore at Mardi Gras.

"*Buenos Noches*," Richardo said to the woman receptionist. "My name is Richardo de la Guarda. I have a reservation. It's for five days."

Putting down her tablet was not something she desired to do. The woman's black name tag had Carol printed. She turned to the computer. "I'll see." She had a small mean mouth with thin lips and chewed gum with more enthusiasm than finding Richardo's reservation. "Yeah, Mr. de la Guarda. I'll need a credit card and some form of identification."

"Certainly. Will my passport do?"

"Yeah." Carol typed without looking away.

Richardo slid his passport and credit card across the black marble counter.

A few keystrokes later, Carol pushed back Richardo's documents and a key card. "Mr. de la Guarda, you are all checked in. You are in Room 374. You can use the elevator over there."

"*Gracias.*" Richardo pocketed his passport. "Is the pool open?"

Carol, who had already turned away and was checking her tablet, said over her shoulder, "Pool's closed for repairs."

Before Richardo could thank her, she'd gone back to her tablet and aggressively chomping her gum.

A faded red oriental carpet lined the hallway. It was ripped and sewn, wrinkled and frayed. Old, light fixtures that were supposed to resemble whale oil lanterns, some not working, most were askew on the walls.

Passing down the hall, Rich heard loud TVs, conversation, a baby wailing and noises associated with producing an infant to join the wailing chorus.

It took a couple of swipes of his card before the door clicked open.

The room, a standard layout of bath, double beds, dresser, desk and TV, conveyed an air of overall weariness. The air conditioner unit under the window hummed, not disturbing the warmth and stuffiness of the room. Rich hooked the chain lock and tossed his satchel on the second bed. He drew the curtain aside. The pool below was empty except for puddles of dirty water. It was fenced all around with yellow caution tape and orange netting. Regardless, there were groups of people gathered drinking and partying.

He lay restless.

There was nothing of interest on TV. He tossed the remote control onto the bed and got up, pacing.

Roitman's face kept coming back to him. This was the third man that participated in killing his wife. Roitman laughed at him. Over and over he plotted how to get his revenge. Rich thought through every form of killing the man: knife, gun, strangulation, bludgeoning. The square-boned Slavic face haunted him. Rich saw Roitman and the others carry Gisele's naked, dead body up the hillside to leave her in the brush. Roitman would pay, dearly.

Pacing.

He needed release.

Pacing.

He needed a drink.

Down the elevator with happy people.

The Captain's Lounge was inside the main casino. Rich dodged down aisles of slots and hopeful gamblers. It took a moment for his eyes to adjust to the dim light in the lounge. A tawdry affair, the Captain's Lounge was kitted out like a sunken ship. The long bar was backlit and nearly empty. Booths and round cocktail tables lined the opposite wall.

Rich sat at a booth with silver duct tape mending a tear in the back of a section.

A middle-aged waitress made up as a serving wench appeared.

"What'll it be, Sugar?"

"*Cerveza.*"

"What kind?"

"I'm not from here. Balboa?"

"Never heard of it."

"Atlas?"

"Nope."

"Soberana?"

"Uh huh."

"Panama?"

"Pacifico?"

"Ahhh, *si*, yes."

"I'll be right back, Hon."

He had to get Roitman out of his brain. He needed sleep for his drive to San Diego tomorrow. And when he did meet Roitman, he needed to be cool and not so keyed up that he might raise Roitman's suspicions.

"Here you go." The waitress placed a bottle on a round cardboard coaster, a glass alongside.

"*Gracias.*"

"Let me know when you need another."

He tilted the glass and poured. Chilled, but not cold, it relaxed him from the first swallow.

A couple laughed from the far end of the bar. He was all over her and she kept looking Rich's way.

He glanced away.

Rich pulled out his burner phone and dialed up The Ordinary. It took a couple of rings but Riku answered.

"The Ordinary."

"Hey, Riku, is Daisy available?" There was noise of people talking and laughing and music in the background.

"Yeah, Keeper. She's working the tables and should be here in a minute."

In a few minutes, Daisy came on the line. "What's up, Boss." She paused. "Where are you?"

"Never mind that. Everything going okay?"

"You had more visitors."

"Visitors?"

"Guys in suits."

"They say who they were?"

"Yeah," Daisy replied. "They had no problem saying."

"Who?"

"U.S. Marshals...with a warrant for you."

"Shit," he breathed out. "What did you tell them?"

"You were out of town and I didn't know when you'd be back."

"Good. Good."

"What kind of trouble are you in now, Boss," Daisy's voice was stern.

"It's nothing." Rich drained his beer. "I can deal with it when I get back."

"These were some serious dudes. You better deal with it."

"Okay, Mom." Rich raised his glass and gave it a refill wiggle.

"Hey, no call for that."

"You're right. I apologize. I'll deal with it. Okay?" He sighed. "Anything else?"

"Nope. Everything running smooth."

"Thank you, Daisy. I don't know what I would do without you."

"Up shit crick, for sure." The young woman paused. "I don't mean to sound freaky, Boss...but...ah, we don't want to get mixed up in what it is you're into. I mean, we, ah...don't want to be considered accomplices."

"You won't."

"Are you sure?"

"As long as you don't know where I am or what's happening, you're in the clear."

"All right, I guess," she reluctantly agreed.

"I'll call in a couple of days."

"Okay, Boss."

The waitress came up with another Pacifico.

The guy at the bar was getting all handsy while the woman continued to stare at Rich.

CHAPTER 10

He woke in his clothes, with a raging headache, a sticky mouth that tasted of stale beer, and someone banging in the hallway outside his room.

A drunk leaned his face heavily against the door to the next room. "C'mon, Baby, lemme in. She meant nothing to me. Honest."

He poked a finger between the curtains. Dawn and neon lights like a hangover battled the day. Showered, dressed Rich became Richardo. He packed his satchel and took the elevator to the lobby. The ringing of bells at the slot machines mingled with vacuum cleaners. His SUV had survived the night unmolested.

"All night pharmacy," he asked the phone.

"Pharmacy on Paradise. Take a right onto East Flamingo."

Rich followed the directions, turning left on Paradise. The pharmacy was bathed in white light. A couple of homeless people were squatting on the side of the building, heads hanging like they were sleeping. Rich entered and walked to the high counter of the pharmacy in the back.

"May I help you?"

"Yes," Rich pulled a pleading face. "I am in a real fix. I'm a diabetic and I left all my needles back at home. Can you help me?"

The white-haired pharmacist studied Rich over his half-glasses, down to the end of his nose. "I can sell you about half a dozen needles, but nothing in quantity."

"That would be great. A real lifesaver. I use a bigger gauge."

"Number 20s?"

"Perfect."

"I can ring you up here." The pharmacist went around to the back.

On the way out, Rich picked up a pair of black gloves.

A couple of turns and merges and Rich was on I-15 leaving Las Vegas in his rearview mirror. He squared himself away for the five-hour drive to Los Angeles and who knows how much more from Los Angeles to San Diego.

A long, monotonous drive through the Mojave Desert to Barstow. He got directions to Los Angeles, knowing he faced the dreaded "Spaghetti Bowl" just east of L.A. Sure enough, traffic clustered and slowed the closer Rich got to Los Angeles. GPS got him through the maze of exits and off-ramps toward San Bernardino. If there were no accidents ahead, Rich should arrive in San Diego by mid-afternoon.

The San Diego airport lay downtown and on the water. Rich weaved through downtown traffic and found the airport Hilton. San Diego seemed like a small town on the coast.

Rich pulled under the entrance awning, pausing a moment. He had to be Richardo from that moment on.

"*Hola*," Richardo said to the attractive, early-twenties woman behind the green marble reception desk.

"My name is Richardo de la Guarda."

"Of course, *Senor* de la Guarda, we've been expecting you." She stopped typing and looked at Richardo. "We have an executive suite reserved for you on the fifth floor. Could I trouble you for a credit card and I.D.? And would you fill this card out?"

"Of course." Richardo fished his passport and credit card out of the inside pocket of his suit jacket.

"Thank you." She typed as she talked. "Will you need help with your bags?" She had a pleasant voice.

"No, *gracias*."

"Valet for your vehicle?"

"No, thank you."

"Okay. Here is your key card." She took the signature card back. "And we are all set." Then she added, "We have a wonderful continental breakfast spread from six-thirty to ten."

"*Gracias*." Richardo collected his documents.

He parked in the rear lot and entered through a back door.

This was definitely an upgrade from the Emigrant Isles. The hallway carpet was plush and accents all in working order, stylish and new.

His suite was classy, a sitting area with a white couch and dresser, mini-bar and a modern bath all glass and upscale features. The bed was in an adjoining room with floor to ceiling windows that looked out upon San Diego Harbor. A

World War Two aircraft carrier was docked to the north of the bay.

"This is more like it," Richardo muttered, placing his satchel on a white upholstered wing chair.

He checked his phone for the time—Three-thirty. He'd wait an hour to call Nudelman. Meanwhile, he hung his brown suit in the bathroom and put the shower on hot. A good steam should take out the wrinkles.

Nerves, like live wires running through his body, had him all jitters in his belly and weak in the knees.

Doubt snuck out of the shadows in the back of his thoughts. What're you doing? he asked himself.

He circled room to room in his suite, head down, pinching his lower lip.

Why? He knew this as well. They killed Gisele. They killed his wife. They killed his wife instead of him.

They will pay. Every last one of them will pay. Time went slowly. Should he call Nudelman now?

No. At four-thirty, and maybe five minutes late. He would be preparing to leave and impatient. That will make Nudelman more agreeable.

Time ran like on a muddy track, slipping, sliding, not moving forward. He'd thought this part all through, changing it now might screw it all up. The nerves, the doubt may cause a misstep and he'd end up dead. Stick with the plan, he told himself.

And if he failed...if he failed...he was prepared for that.

He laid out his brown suit from the shower steam. He polished his tight Oxfords with a towel. Shirt, bolo tie, gloves, all ready.

Finally, the digital clock tripped four-thirty.

The line at the other end rang once, twice three times.

"Nudelman Luxury Real Estate," a woman with a distinct Eastern European accent said.

"Is *Senor* Nudelman available," Richardo asked.

"Who's calling?" she wanted to know.

"Richardo del la Guarda. He said for me to call him."

"Hold, please."

Cheesy music off a poorly turned receiver played.

"De la Guarda," a man's gruff voice suddenly answered. "Are you in town?" He also had a trace of an accent.

"*Si*...you said to call."

"Yes, but I was hoping for earlier in the day." Though gruff, Richardo detected a weakness in Nudelman's voice.

"May we meet, *Senor?*"

"Ahhhhhhh." He's stalling for time, Richardo thought.

"Yeah, I suppose."

"Is good...I am here for a couple of days just."

"Do you know where our office is located?"

"*Si*...ehhhh...no."

"We're on...."

"No problem. I find with GPS."

Rush hour in San Diego was more an exercise in getting out of the way of people hurrying for houses in the outlying suburbs than people coming into town for dinner or sports or a show.

San Diego is a town that is easy to find the way around.

Richardo found Nudelman's Real Estate on a coast road. A white siding and big green glass geometric building with a small parking area out front. The light inside burned bright inside. Richardo thought it best to park on the street and not in the lot. That way, Nudelman and Roitman would not be able to ID his SUV. He circled the block finding a parking space up the street.

Richardo parked, got out and slipped on his suit jacket, glasses, fedora and black gloves. He snatched the "salted" leather-bound attaché case, leaving the duplicate on the passenger side and locking the SUV.

The sun hung inches above the curve of the ocean's horizon. A nice walk with a warm breeze at his shoulders. The ocean on his left and some pricey homes on his right. Noisy gulls hung nearly motionless on the cliffside updrafts.

The orange sun shined off the glass of Nudelman Real Estate as Richardo turned in the parking lot and approached the tall glass doors in the center of the building.

He clutched the attaché case to his chest and struggled with the heavy doors.

"*Hola*," he smiled and said to an older, big-boned, bob-haired woman at a desk just inside the entry. "I...I am Richardo de la Guarda here to see Mr. Nudelman."

The woman rose. "Please sit and I will inform Mr. Nudelman."

She had an accent. It was the woman from the phone.

"*Gracias*," he said to her fat back stuffed into a too-short yellow shift.

Richardo spotted Roitman on a cell phone at a desk outside what must've been Nudelman's center back office.

A hot wave of hate swept up his spine. He took a deep breath and let it out his nose slowly, calming himself for the moment.

The office had three rows of desks, about nine in all. These were agent's desks and they led to a row of three large offices at the back. Aside from Roitman, no other agents were present. Roitman's desk was to the side of a large frosted glass office in the middle and what seemed a store-room with printer and shelves to the other side. The walls were decorated with large framed photos of houses mixed with the usual Hotel Coronado, ballpark and zoo pictures. The raised letters on the wall at the back office read: Nudelman Real Estate, and below it: A Cozmos Company. A smell of pine could be detected throughout the office.

The woman walked back. "Mr. Nudelman will see you."

"The office in the back? Center?" Richardo asked knowing the answer.

"Yeah," her impatience came out in the curtness of a quick response.

He got up clumsily, almost dropping the attaché case. He walked to the back with a short, painful stride due to tight shoes. In the periphery of his sight, Richardo noted Roitman's eyes following him.

A short, round-shouldered overweight man crouched over his desk, flanked by piles of folders. He glanced up, and seeing Richardo in the doorway started to cough.

"*Senor* Nudelman." Richardo waited for Nudelman's cough to subside.

"Y-Yes," he said in the last waning hacks. "Mr....de la Guarda. Sit, please." He waved to a pair of chairs on the other side of the desk.

"Sorry." Nudelman plucked a tissue from a box, spit something into the middle of the tissue, wiped his hands and dropped the balled-up paper into a waste can. He reached over the desk to shake hands.

Richardo raised his gloved hands. "*Perdon, Senor* ...germs."

"Ahhh," Nudelman replied in his growling voice. "I did wonder why."

"Are you ill, *Senor*?" Richardo settled himself in a chair and placed the attaché case and fedora on the second chair.

"No...bum ticker."

"I am very sorry."

"No more than me, Mr. de la Guarda." Nudelman pulled a manila folder from a stack on his desk. It had Richardo de la Guarda with a question mark written on it.

"I've taken the liberty of pulling some listings and flyers based on our email conversation last week." He turned the open folder around and pushed it over to Richardo. "These listings are within your price and location requests."

"*Si.*" Richardo read carefully, turning the printed pages over. He tapped one. "Ahhh, yes, this one I like very much."

"That listing is signed to my associate Mr. Roitman. He will show it to you."

"Good."

"Mr. Roitman is here. Let me bring him in, and we can set up an appointment." He picked up the phone and punched a number.

Richardo smiled, while inside, he was steeling himself to face Roitman.

"Symon, could you come in here?" Nudelman hung up the phone. "He's finishing up a call and will be in momentarily."

"Good...good." Richardo continued to leaf through the print outs in the folder. "I like this also."

"I'll put that one down for a tour."

"You need me." Roitman stood at the end of the desk. Richardo did not look up.

"Symon. This is Richardo de la Guarda from Panama," he paused. "It was Panama, wasn't it?'

Richardo raised his eyes. "Panama City."

"Symon is my top producer."

And killer, thought Richardo as he stood, holding out a gloved hand.

The square-boned, broad forehead and flat Slavic face tried to look friendly but failed with a small lipless mouth. Roitman saw Richardo's gloved hand and visibly balked.

"Germophobe, Symon."

"Oh."

He also had a taint of an accent, more German than Eastern European. They shook hands.

Richardo gripped Roitman's limp hand hard. "A pleasure to meet you, *Senor* Roitman."

The other man's expression clouded over. His small mouth tensed. His eyes narrowed. "Yes...pleasure." His forehead wrinkled. "Have we met before?"

Sweat blossomed at Richardo's temples. "Have you ever been to Panama City?"

"No."

"I've not been to Germany, but we have many Germans in Central America."

Symon's face showed traces of anger. "Nor have I."

"Oh? No? My error. You sound so German." He had anticipated this happening and turned the tables on Roitman.

"I..." Roitman started but was held up by Nudelman.

"You will be showing Mr. de la Guarda some listings. He is very interested in your Ocean Side property."

Roitman was almost fuming, but folded his hand behind his back, looked down at the floor and rocked on his heels. "Certainly," he softly muttered.

"Thank you, Symon."

"It was nice meeting you," Richardo said.

He grunted a reply, smiling to the doorway, frowning on the way out.

"Sit, Mr. de la Guarda. Refresh my memory on your background." Nudelman leaned back in his tall leather chair and laced his fingers over his ample belly. He coughed intermittently. "If we're going to work together, I will need to start a file." The round man put his hands on the desktop and pushed himself up, out of his chair. "I assume you have identification."

"Oh, course." Richardo reached for his attaché case. "Will my passport do?"

"Usually does." Nudelman struggled to gain his breath.

Richardo opened the case and turned it so Nudelman could get a good look inside.

There were ten banded stacks of greenbacks each topped with a thousand-dollar bill. Nudelman's eyes focused.

"Are thousand-dollar bills still in circulation?"

"Yes, but they are rare."

"That's a helluva lot of money to be walking around with."

Handing over his passport, Richardo shrugged. "I have a lot of money."

"It might be wise for you to leave your attaché case in my office safe." Nudelman did not take his eyes off the inside of the case.

He's pegged me as a real rube, Richardo thought.

"How much money do you have in there?"

"You see."

Richardo could tell he was counting in his head. "What? Close to a million?"

"*Si*, probably."

"Tell me again?" Nudelman shambled to the print room with Richardo's passport. "How do you know me?"

"A friend of yours in a Guatemalan prison." Richardo paused. "He told an acquaintance of mine if I wanted to clean and move my money you were the *hombre* to see."

Handing back Richardo's passport, Nudelman collapsed into his leather seat. "I am never going to get rid of that *Baystryuk.*"

"Feinberg?"

"Yes." He opened and wrote on a manila folder. "How come I've never heard of you?"

"I'm very careful."

The large receptionist leaned into the doorway. "I'm leaving now."

"Okay, Yelena. See you in the morning."

Richardo dropped his passport into his attaché case and put it on the chair. Nudelman had fallen for it. The stacks that appeared to be thousands were all fives and ones topped by a single thousand-dollar bill.

"You don't have much of an accent for a Panamanian."

"*Mi Madre*, she is Panamanian, petite, beautiful with masses of long black hair, pale skin and true Spanish beauty."

"Doesn't explain it."

"Popi was an American from Utah. He worked as an engineer and we lived in the canal zone." Richardo went on. "I went to American schools and my running mates were American kids. We spoke mostly English at home."

"Okay." Nudelman put listing flyers in the folder. "Makes sense. Forgive my curiosity, but how'd you get your money?"

Richardo sighed, settling back in his chair. "...is long story."

"I'm all ears."

"I worked on the canal since I was sixteen. I noticed some containers were handled differently. Those came down from the hills. I thought they were bananas or other tropical fruit."

Nudelman coughed and coughed. "I...I got you."

"We broke into a couple and found it was more than bananas." Richardo toyed with his fedora. "With a little grease to the container loaders, we got word to the owners of the containers that if they wanted their cargo loaded, it would cost them."

Nudelman chuckled. "Bet I know the response."

"*Si*. They sent down a truckload of armed *hombres*."

A trace of a smile crossed the fleshy face of the real estate broker.

"We notified the Federales that Contras were coming down from the hills to take over the canal." Richardo laughed. "They were met by the military and after a fierce gun battle turned back."

"Smart."

"Soon after, a car came down the jungle road with the money."

"Good scheme. Can't imagine it would last."

"It didn't. I recruited more buddies and we started to hold the containers ransom. The drug lords realized that was cheaper to pay us and get their cargo to Galveston, Houston or New Orleans than fight with us."

"They had to be out to get you."

"They were, but remember, I said I was careful. They had no idea who I was and who was in my crew." Richardo took a breath. "I study. I learn from *The Godfather*, *Scarface*, and *Goodfellas*—the flashy, mouthy *hombre* is the one that is killed or arrested."

"Took a lot of bribes to keep this all quiet, I imagine."

"Yeah....but well worth it. Nobody knew it was us," Richardo dropped his fedora on the attaché case. "Once you accept that everybody wants a little of your blood—then your business runs smooth. And anyone in my crew that started to spend or look like they have money or drive a fancy car—he was gone."

"What'd you do with the money?"

"Couldn't bank it. I bought a warehouse and set up a paper company—Isthmus Import & Export. I have a warehouse full of Yankee greenbacks."

"And an attaché case with a million bucks. You got anyone that can verify all this?"

Richardo brought out a card with the contact he'd bought from his lawyer Borodavka. "Call this number and ask about me."

Nudelman squinted at the card. "I'll do it now."

"Don't bother. That's a government number and no one will be there."

"Okay...you need to move your money."

"I need to clean it."

"Well, don't know how we can help."

Richardo let out a big laugh. "Don't play cutesy pie with me. I will give you both ends—buyer and seller—representing me. What percent do you get?"

"Well, usually fifteen percent."

"You will double that when I buy a couple of houses."

"Maybe."

Richardo laughed again. "I didn't consider this from someone who made their pile during the Russian Privatization after the Soviet Union collapse."

Nudelman's face turned to stone.

"You were one of the Kleptocrats, stashing money in Swiss bank accounts."

"And you could do the same."

"I said I was careful. Very suspicious for a Panamanian who lives in a modest house in Ocean Reef to be traveling to Zurich and consorting with bankers."

"So, you want to turn over real estate."

"For an import business, it's not so much a red flag." Richardo leaned forward. "Not like selling women or putting your money on the wrong horse in the Yeltsin/Putin race."

Nudelman grimly nodded. "What're your plans?"

Richardo gathered a huge breath. "You no see? Okay, I tell you. The houses are baby steps and I test you. We buy, we sell, we put money in paper company—Ithmus Acquisition. That company buys office buildings in Los Angeles, San Francisco, Chicago, Toronto, Boston and New York."

Nudelman arched an eyebrow.

"You are impressed," Richardo continued. "Each of my loyal crew run shadow company—this Ithmus Import as the parent. Then they can spend and live with no red flag from the law. I see a long time ago my amigos think women and drugs the peak. No, no...women and drugs the start, then get out as fast as you can."

The two men looked at each other in silence.

"I say too much," Richardo finally added. "But once Ithmus Imports she have office buildings, we set up bank, auto finance, insurance and what-all. All totally legit. No? Then we do an IPO." Richardo laughed.

Nudelman shifted in his chair, stifling a cough. "Maybe you buy Cosmoz." The round-shouldered man jerked his thumb to the sign behind him.

"No chance," Richardo shook his head. "I hear the general killed himself."

"Where did you hear that?"

"I hear a lot. Irina, his daughter, was blown up in India."

"Suka...yeah. She trafficked in women in Chicago."

"Then I hear the crazy boy, Nicky, was gunned down in a bar fight in Saint Louis."

"That you got a little wrong. It was Omaha. That one you thought was German, Symon, he might end up running Cosmoz...unless..."

"No, not me."

"Why do you want to use me to buy your houses?"

"I just want to work with you."

"Okay." The broker struggled up, hand out.

They shook. Richardo also stood, taking up his attaché case.

"Maybe we go eat now. Where can we get some *ceviche*?"

"I would have no idea. Shall we meet tomorrow and look over some properties?"

"I have meetings in the morning and afternoon. We can meet in the evening."

"Whatever works," Nudelman led Richardo through the office.

Richardo noticed Roitman had left.

"I'll call you time for us to meet," Richardo paused at the glass door. "I don't need to see all the properties. We need houses that sell fast."

"Let me handle that." Nudelman looked at the card. "And I will call to confirm you are who you say you are."

"*Buenas noches*," Richardo tipped his hat.

"Yeah." Nudelman coughed hard. He tried once more. "I still don't think you should be carrying that case around. Not with all that money."

"Ahhh, it'll be fine," Richardo waved him off.

Richardo hustled back to the parked SUV, past a couple walking a dog, and retrieved the empty, duplicate attaché case. It had no weight. He needed something to give it some heft. Rummaging through his satchel he found an old pair of running shoes. Tossing the shoes into the case, he thumped closed the brass clasps.

Running back to the office, he held the case cross-armed as if he had the first case with its *million* in Yankee dollars. Meeting Nudelman at the glass door locking up, Richardo said to him: "I use my second mind and she say you right. I don't trust the hotel safe. I'll put the attaché case in your safe. If that's okay?"

Nudelman struggled to suppress a smile. "Fine. It'll be safe here." Richardo led the bulky man to his office. "We'll lock her up safe as milk." His hand lay benevolently on Richardo's shoulder. "You're doing the right thing."

Nudelman spun the tumbler and opened the safe. He reached for Richardo's attaché case.

"Oh no, I'll do it," Richardo said.

Nudelman watched Richardo slide the case into the safe.

Walking down the block, Richardo met the young couple walking a black and white Boston Terrier. He stopped.

"May I pet your dog?"

"Certainly."

He stooped and held out the back of his hand for the terrier to sniff.

"He seems to like you."

"I had a Boston Terrier."

"Had?"

"He was killed." Richardo scratched behind the dog's upraised ears. "What's his name?"

"Zeppo." The couple exchanged smiles.

"I get it. Great name."

"What was your dog's name?"

"Roommate."

"Oh, I like that."

"I miss that dog." Richardo rose. "Have a nice evening."

"You as well."

CHAPTER 11

Richardo walked out of the mirror and stainless steel elevator with designs on a late breakfast at the hotel grille. Crossing the white mottled marble and white wood lobby, Richardo caught some movement out of the corner of his eye.

He saw a large man put the quarter-folded newspaper on another chair and rise.

Richardo stopped at the receptionist's desk. "Any messages for me?"

"Your name?"

"Richardo de la Guarda."

The man paused at a display and fingered through various brochures for tourist sites in and around San Diego.

He measured probably six-foot, with broad-shoulders and distended belly that spilled over the sides of his hips. Not physically fit: although he had a boxer's look about him like he could handle himself in a pinch.

Richardo started to move away from the reception desk, and the man mimicked him.

His face had seen a few punch-ups, judging by the drooping of his features, flattened cheekbone and scrambled nose. That nose must've often been on the receiving end of a bunch of knuckles. It appeared spread all over the center of his unflattering mug. A thick head of coarse black hair meant he was young at some point in his life. A tired-looking black suit hung off his broad shoulders as it would a misshaped coat hanger in the closet.

Richardo wandered from reception to the grille.

The man followed, pretending to read from a San Diego Zoo brochure.

What a lousy tail, Richardo thought. Does he care he's that obvious?

A waiter, in a mock tuxedo and long apron tied at the waist, met Richardo at the door. He directed him to a small bistro table with wire-backed chairs in the middle of the grille. When the waiter went to seat the man in the black, Richardo changed tables to one along the sidewall.

The waiter, absentmindedly, motioned for the man to take a seat at the table Richardo vacated. His voice was slurry, guttural and annoyed thanking the waiter, and he sat facing Richardo.

A plate of scrambled eggs, Richardo ordered, with sliced tomatoes, bacon and sausage, and a side of fruit. He added, "Café American."

'Pardon?"

"Coffee, milk and sugar."

"Ah, certainly."

Who did he belong to, Richardo wondered. Roitman? That made more sense than Nudelman. Nudelman was more interested in selling houses to Richardo. And besides, he was sick, physically ill, and knew it. Roitman may have recognized Richardo and put the tail on him just to see if he checked out. They were still grifters, though, and Roitman would benefit—he could only be looking out for the organization.

The man ordered loudly—"Toast, butter, grape jelly and coffee."

Richardo pulled out his burner phone and feigned a series of phone calls. He noticed the Tail leaned toward him and strained to hear the conversation. Hungry, he relished his breakfast, eating fast from the plate on the side and talking with his mouth full.

The cup of coffee and toast kept coming, again and again. This went on until the lunch crowd began to gather at the entrance. It got to him, all the coffee.

Richardo had his head down, but a subtle eye on the man.

He had to get up and head to the lavatory.

Quickly, Richardo flipped a twenty-dollar bill from the thick fold in his pocket. He stood and got the waiter's attention, pointing to the bill on the table. The waiter acknowledged with a nod. And Richardo elbowed through the luncheon set and was through the hotel lobby before the Tail had returned from the toilet.

With a quick step, Richardo went out into the sunny Southern California midday, walking briskly half a block down, then ducking into the doorway of a jeweler.

Not a moment after, the dark suit came out of the hotel in a dash, looking left and right, visibly frantic.

Richardo had him fixed in the reflection of the jewelry display window.

The Tail started up the street at a half-jog coming toward Richardo. He opened the jewelry store door just as the dark suit neared and went past. The poor guy went up the block with eyes searching like a puppy separated from his person.

"May I help you, Sir?" a young man, lean-looking, with neatly trimmed chin beard and slicked-back hair, asked.

Richardo half-turned. "Yes, a croissant and cappuccino."

"Pardon?"

The Tail jaywalked from across the street and went into the parking garage.

"Oh, my error. I thought this a brasserie."

Richardo heard an indignant huff behind him as he left the jewelry store and followed the Tail into the parking garage. He stood in the shadow of a large square concrete column and watched the Tail go to his SUV. Obviously, he did not know Richardo's rental or he would've looked to see if he left the hotel.

He inched around the column as the Tail exited.

The Tail turned left.

Hustling to his SUV, Richardo jumped into the driver's seat. He hit contacts on his phone.

"Mr. Nudelman," Richardo said over the sound of traffic at the exit. "I know we planned to see properties this afternoon—but I have last-minute appointments and probably won't get there until later. Like after six o'clock. That work?"

"That'll be okay. I will wait." Nudelman replied. "Oh, I called your contact in the Panamanian government."

"*Si*, and what did he say?"

Nudelman chuckled, then coughed nearly choking. "He said you were *one bad hombre.*"

"I tell you that."

"See you later."

"*Si*...we do good business tonight."

Nudelman was thinking of the likelihood of a multi-million-dollar score, buying three or four houses to turn quickly. Anything Richardo wanted, he would comply with.

Richardo needed to separate Nudelman and Roitman. He could not deal with both at the same time. That was not part of the plan.

They merged onto I-5 and Richardo let the shadow have a three-car lead and over one lane, staying in his blind spot. "Now, I'm your tail."

They headed downtown. Traffic was light, so it was easy for Richardo to stay close enough.

"Where we going, *Amigo*—the ballpark? It's not baseball season."

He slipped into the exiting lane and turned off I-5 onto Broadway—heading to Gaslamp Quarter.

"I've seen the USS Midway."

They shunted along Broadway, the cars congesting block after block.

Richardo gave him enough of a lead he should not have been spotted.

The SUV had its blinker on to turn left onto Sixth Ave.

Richardo twisted his head right and left to make sure it was clear to turn. He got in two cars behind the shadow.

The shadow slowed and parked in the middle of the block. Richardo, staring straight ahead, drove past. The Tail opened his driver's side door.

"What's this?" he muttered, parking up the block.

The Tail had parked a few storefronts past Pushin's Russian Restaurant & Bar. Richardo was opposite Bucadi Beppo Restaurant, close to the G Street intersection. He adjusted his rearview mirror. The black suit got out, lit-up a smoke and lounged against the fender of his SUV. A minute later, out from Pushin's, came three men. No surprise, between a pair of black tracksuit thugs, stood Roitman.

Roitman did most of the talking, and from his body language, it was not an exchange of pleasantries. Roitman gestured his arms wildly and thrust his face forward. The larger man hung his head.

Richardo thought, makes sense he put a dog on me, especially if he had the slightest suspicion he knew me. He imagined what Roitman spit into the other man's face. "*Arschloch*—I tell you follow him and don't let him out of your sight. And you lose him...*blod blod blod.*"

Back at the hotel room, Richardo unpacked his satchel of the Ephedra powder, syringes and purple rubber gloves. In the bathroom, he laid out the ingredients on the marble counter. He checked the contents of the Ephedra for the potentially lethal ephedrine. Yup, he had the right stuff.

He snapped on the gloves and unscrewed the cap. Carefully he spooned two tablespoons of the brownish powder into a plastic cup, then slowly filled it under the dribbling tap to about half. Nearly all the powder dissolved, but the buffering agent. He swirled it around and spooned off the non-liquid floating at the top.

In a second cup, he also put in two tablespoons of Ephedra, filled with an equal amount of water. He dissolved as much as he could.

Opening the box of insulin syringes, he took out a pair, tore open the paper wrapper, and laid them on a folded face towel.

He poured the Ephedra from the second cup into the first—doubling the dosage.

Putting a large wad of cotton on the top, Richardo let the Ephedra seep through.

He snapped open the protective orange needle cover on a syringe and pulled in 10cc's of Ephedra into the syringe. Careful still, he capped the syringe. There appeared enough of the deadly liquid remaining. Richardo filled a second syringe. Both syringes he put in a hard plastic case and set aside.

He sighed, not realizing how much he had sweat and wiped his face with a towel hanging off a hook on the door.

Now he needed to clean up. He dumped the remaining Ephedra in the cups into the toilet and flushed. He rinsed out the cups and put them in a plastic bag. With the face towel, he screwed on the cap of the Ephedra and wiped down the bottle. Using an alcohol-wet towelette, he went over the counter and facets and around the sink. With the gloves still on, Richardo went to the bedroom and put the bottle of Ephedra and syringes in his satchel, the alcohol towel, and packaging into the plastic bag. He snapped off the purple gloves last and tied the top of the plastic bag.

"Ready," Richardo whispered.

No. He did a thorough wipe-down of the room wearing purple rubber gloves, wielding a wad of antiseptic pads. Moving quickly around the room, he wiped the patio doors, handle and windows, the television remote—all the buttons, the smooth marble top of the dresser, all wall switches, door handles and light switches. He knew it would not prevent forensics from finding something to trace him by—but it would buy him time. And he needed time. Then he went into the bathroom for a second wipe down.

Richardo packed everything into plastic bags.

He lay on the bed, propped up the pillows and waited.

Pocketing the key card on his way out, he pulled his sleeve over his hand and closed the door.

He smiled at the CCTV in the hallway. He flashed a cheeky grin at the CCTV in the elevator. He nodded to the CCTV red light in the lobby and waved at the receptionist.

Wiped out, he put "paid" to the hotel and slipped out a side door to the parking garage.

CHAPTER 12

Afterward, Richardo went down to Dog Beach. He dropped the plastic bag of syringe wrappers, the plastic cups he blended the lethal Ephedra concoction in, and the wash-rag and spoon he mixed it with into the dented, rusty, seamed green barrel most people used to throw away their dogshit. He sat in the cool sand under a warm sun and watched the dogs play in ocean waves. Gradually, the sun turned orange, and Richardo waited until the horizon took a sizeable bite out of the orb. He went over to Ocean Beach and munched on half a turkey sandwich outside a cafe. Killing time. Everything he did distracted him from what was at hand for tonight.

By the time he parked outside of Nudelman's Real Estate, it was well past dark and the city lights were high.

"My apologies *Senor* Nudelman," Richardo said, bumbling into the office. "I had so many meetings this afternoon I lose track of time."

"Not a problem, *Senor* de la Guarda," the round man beckoned. "Come into my office."

There was no one else in the office.

They settled in. "Have you had a chance to look over the properties and make some choices?" Nudelman got out the flyers and a stack of San Diego houses in play.

"I have." Richardo took out a notebook. He scanned the scribbling, pinching his lower lip. "I like the one on 4th Street at A Avenue in Coronado that lists for one million nine hundred and eighty thousand dollars. I'd pay the asking price on that."

"Why?" Nudelman found the listing one-sheet and made a note.

"Close to the beach."

"And there's another on Camden Court for nine hundred, eighty-six thousand, nine hundred dollars. It was built in 2018 and near Camino del Norte. Very nice, clean."

"There are more affordable units."

"Not interested in affordable."

"Okay. I will make a note."

"Remember...we offer asking price. We don't want to argue about price. Got it?"

"Got it."

"Another is in Monaco, with an ocean view."

"How much?"

"One million, seven hundred and fifty thousand dollars."

"I like the Ocean Boulevard house."

"That's five point five million dollars. That might be too rich for your blood."

"Too rich? I told you," Richardo laughed. "I have a warehouse full of greenbacks. I'll pay cash."

Nudelman wrote and sighed. "Oh-kay." He put his pen down. "That listing is my agent Roitman's. I'll have to refer you to him."

"I'd rather work with you."

"You are...in a way."

"Roitman is a strange name."

"It's German, with a touch of Ukrainian. I'll put you two together when the time's right."

"Certainly." Richardo tapped the flyers with his gloved finger on the edge on the desk. It was time to pull the string on the con. "I plan to put together the down payments from the cash in my attaché case. That's in your safe."

"Makes sense."

"Let's get the case out and start divvying up the money."

Nudelman spun the black dial and quickly did the combination safe. There was a click on the heavy door and the safe opened. He pulled the case from the shelf inside the safe. He turned, holding the case with a queer look on his face.

Grinning, Richardo took the case. "Now we can do some real business," he said excitedly.

Nudelman sunk down to his executive chair.

Richardo snapped open the case. It opened—empty--but for a beat-up pair of running shoes.

"W-Where's my money?"

"What?"

Richardo spun the case around. "My money? It's gone."

"Impossible."

"Look."

"There has to be a mistake."

"This is my case. Here, these are my initials. Shoes? It's empty. Where's my money?"

"I'm sure it's safe."

"Safe? No, it not. It's gone. I want my money."

"I think maybe Symon, Mr. Roitman, might've mistakenly taken the wrong case."

"With my money?"

"I will call him." Nudelman took up his phone and clicked on his contact. No answer. It went to voice mail. Nudelman turned away. "Symon. Call me."

"My money? Where is it?"

"It's safe, I am sure. There's just been a mix-up." Nudelman started to sweat.

"Safe? Safe? It's gone. What happened to my money?"

"I'll get it."

"There was over a million dollars in the case. Now it disappear." Richardo held up a shoe. "Where'd it go?" Richardo rose, raising his voice. "A million dollars."

"It's okay."

"It's not here."

"I'll get it." Nudelman mopped his brow. "I just need to talk to Mr. Roitman."

"Call him again, dammit."

"I'll get it."

"Get it now." It was time for Richardo to ratchet up the tension. "You want I should call my people?"

"No, no, no." Nudelman eyed his open safe. Richardo knew the real estate broker probably had papers and money in the safe he did not want to get in the hands of Richardo's Panamanian's people.

"My money?" Richardo leaned over the desk and said slow and emphatically, "Where's...my...money?"

Nudelman tried Roitman's number again. No answer—again. He left another frantic voice message.

"I am not happy." Richardo started to walk back and forth, banging the sole of the shoe on his palm, very agitated. "And you...will not be happy if I bring my crew up to find my cash." He paused. "You understand, Mr. Nudelman?"

"Hold on, *Senor* de la Guarda." Nudelman was sweating profusely and breathing shallowly. "We'll work this out." The out of shape man searched behind the safe, in the small office, around his desk and all over his office. "You saw me put the case in the safe. You did."

"I thought that I did. But my money—is gone. You turn my money into old shoes." Richardo pulled out his phone. "I'm going to call an associate...now. He can be here in fifteen minutes."

"No, no, there's no need for that. Trust me."

"Trust you? You stole my money."

"Put the phone down. Let's be reasonable."

"Reasonable? I want my million dollars." Richardo seemed to steam. "What are you going to do to get my money back?"

"Get your money back?"

"Yes, my money. I want it back now. You going to replace my money?"

"Replace?"

"I'll call my associate."

Nudelman had a tough time catching his breath. "No...what do you want?"

"I want money...my money."

"Maybe...maybe I can front you some money until we get your briefcase back."

"All my money?"

Nudelman went to the safe. "I don't have that kind of cash on hand."

"What do you have—more shoes?"

He had to stop and let his breath catch up. Nudelman fanned through a couple of stacks of bills. "I have...about...four hundred thousand dollars."

"Oh yeah, you give me four hundred thousand dollars and steal my million dollars. That a fair deal?"

"I didn't take your million dollars."

"You no get me my money in an hour," Richardo said through clenched teeth. "I will kill you...slow."

A shocked expression spread across the broker's pasty face.

"I'm sure Mr. Roitman has it...by accident." Nudelman took off his suit coat jacket. The armpits on his dress shirt were soaked. "Listen. Listen. I will front you four hundred thousand dollars. I just need to get in touch with Symon. I am sure he has your attaché case by accident."

"Oh yeah," Richardo spit out. He slipped his free hand into his suit jacket pocket like he gripped something with a wood handle and iron barrel. "I think you con me out of my money."

"No, it's nothing like that."

"Then where my money?" Richardo slammed the shoe hard onto the desk.

Nudelman jumped. "Here...here," the older man took a manila envelope out of the safe and started to stuff stacks of money into it. "This is four hundred thousand dollars.

Maybe more. You hold it until we get your attaché case back." He handed the bulging envelope to Richardo. Richardo threw it on the desk.

"You give me four hundred thousand and take my million?"

"We'll get your money back."

"I still call my associate."

"Don't." Nudelman dialed Roitman's number. No answer. Again, it went to voice mail. "Symon...," he said in a shaky voice. "Did you take the attaché case from the safe? It's Mr. de la Guarda's. He needs it." He fell to his chair, his head in his hands.

"You con me, this I know." Richardo came around behind Nudelman.

"I didn't con you." There was a hint of whining and despair in Nudelman's voice. He tried to turn his head around.

Richardo took the hypodermic from his pocket and flipped open the orange cap.

"*Senor* de la Guarda, I will get your money back, I promise you."

Richardo slammed Nudelman's head down on the desk, pinning it under his hand. With his thumb on the plunger of the hypo, Richardo stabbed the needle into Nudelman's fatty neck. He depressed the plunger down.

"Ow...what're you doing?"

In his real voice, Rich said, "That's for my wife."

Within seconds Nudelman's face went red all over and seemed to expand. He choked and lost his breath. He struggled and tried to get to his feet.

Richardo whacked him hard on the head with the shoe, having to use both hands to hold his head down on the desk.

He threw the hypodermic. It stuck in the wall like a barroom dart.

Nudelman growled and fought to get his hands under the desk. The desk flipped forward and crashed against the opposite wall. Papers flew. The older man spit white froth and wheeled on Richardo. His face had gone from red to purple; his eyes wide open with rage, his nose bled.

Richardo backed away—this was not the reaction he thought he would get from the Ephedra.

Nudelman came after him.

Richardo threw the shoe and it bounced off Nudelman's forehead.

"I knew there was something...something not right about you," the older man choked out.

Richardo jabbed with his left, knocking Nudelman's head back. He kept coming. Richardo knew he would have to bring more meat to stop him. A roundhouse right staggered the broker. Blood trickled from his mouth. But he regained his stance and went for Richardo. Another hard righthand knocked him back, throwing a curved line of blood across the wall.

Papers fluttered about the office, falling to the floor.

His gloves, wet with blood, made a sopping sound with each punch Richardo landed.

The capillaries in the whites of Nudelman's eyeballs burst and tears of bloody rage streamed from his eyes.

Then, he stopped. The look on his purple face changed from anger to alarm. His eyes focused past Richardo. Both hands went to his chest. He groaned, seized and struggled to get his breath. He went down like a bag of wet cement—a goner.

The office became quiet.

"What the hell was that?" Richardo said, breathing heavily.

Richardo worked quickly, pulling the attaché case from under the desk. He tossed the shoes and manila envelope into the case and rifled through the safe. He pulled the hypo dart from the wall and threw it in the case. Just as he was about to turn off the lights to the office, he spotted Nudelman's phone. He scooped it up. Luckily it had not yet shut down. He bit the finger of the glove on his right hand and swiped on the texts to Roitman.

Greaser boy got A LOT of money. A LOT.

Roitman replied with: *We scam him?*

I raised prices on all those listings.

We can sell him all the turds we can't move.

There's a lot of homeless in that area.

The last text from Roitman read: *Yeah. Gotcha. Shame if something happened to him.*

Richardo shut off the lights in the office and hustled out. He drove out to Roitman's Ocean Boulevard property. He went to the phone settings and changed the password in case it might lock him out. He drove past the property. The house was vacant. Parking on the street behind the house Richardo texted Roitman.

Greaser wants to see the Ocean Boulevard prop. He's on his way.

Taking the easement between two houses, Richardo clambered over the stucco fence into the backyard of the Ocean Boulevard house. He tangled himself in a hedge on the other side. Rolling out of the hedge Richardo stopped short, at the rim of an empty kidney-shaped swimming pool.

Getting up, dusting off, Richardo looked around. The house was a block and glass two-story contemporary structure. There were small LED lights on in all floors. He started to move closer to the house, stopping, realizing there might be an alarm system or cameras. Richardo stayed in the shadows on the edge of the backyard.

A blue light filled a second-story window in the house next door. Classic rock music played from somewhere in the block of houses.

Headlights flashed on the side of a house. A car pulled into the front drive of the property.

Richardo froze.

Someone banged against garbage cans alongside the house. It wouldn't be Roitman, he'd have the code for the lockbox on the front door and would get the key.

Who was this?

Richardo crouched low and went to the corner of the fence, by the gate.

Whoever was out there tried the gate latch and found it locked. A grunting attempt to vault the fence loudly failed. He dragged a garbage can to the fence.

Who is this? Richardo wondered.

Straining at the top of the fence, Ricardo recognized it was the Tail that had followed him that morning. The big guy seemed stuck, his suit jacket snagged on the fence.

Richardo held his hand over his mouth rather than be heard snickering at the Tail's dilemma.

Something fell out of the man's pocket and clattered across the brick patio.

"*Chort vse tse,*" Tail hissed.

Richardo seized the opportunity and rose quickly from the shadows. He grabbed Tail's suit coat pulling him over the fence. The large man landed awkwardly, his head banging against a patio step.

While Tail lay there groggy, Richardo felt around in the dark and found an MP-443 Grach Russian-made 9mm automatic with a short silencer that had been loosened from Tail's pocket. When he turned back, Tail stood, a bit rocky, but once on his feet squared up like a boxer.

He was a fighter, Richardo realized.

They parried with fists, moving around. Richardo seemed small facing the thick and much larger man. He knew Tail was regaining his strength quickly. Slipping punches, Richardo walked Tail back. He snorted from his nose with each swing. Richardo let him come on.

Something like a tree limb rocked Richardo. The patio rolled under his feet. White lights flashed before Richardo's eyes. Tail had connected. Pain like the worst headache Richardo ever had, made him woozy. The inside of his mouth seemed like raw hamburger meat. He needed to count his teeth. He shook his head to get his senses back.

In the half-light, Richardo saw Tail kick out. He managed to turn aside and snatch Tail's foot. Twisting it hard, it had the effect to turn tail on the Tail—making him hop off-balance on one foot at the edge of the empty pool.

Richardo pushed Tail's foot up and kicked his leg out from under him.

The big man landed hard on his hip, at the rim and then went head-first into the deep end of the pool. Richardo didn't know if he was dead or knocked cold. He clambered down the ladder and jumped to the rounded bottom. Sound echoed in the empty pool. He could hear rhythmic breathing. Tail lay, unconscious. Richardo took the man's oversized head in the crook of his elbow and, with his free hand, snapped Tail's neck. He heard it crack.

In his pockets, he found an extra magazine for the automatic, filching the dead man's wallet and keys.

CHAPTER 13

Car headlights threw white light over the back yard and neighboring houses.

"Who is this?" Richardo whispered. "Roitman?"

He grappled up the ladder and out of the pool. Moving swiftly, Rich crossed the yard to the shadowy corner by the gate.

Lights started flipping on in the house, living room, dining room and the kitchen.

Richardo spied Roitman moving through the house.

"Dimitri," Richardo heard Roitman say inside the house. "Dimitri?"

His head pounded, but he kept his cool and waited.

The lock on the patio doors snapped open. Exterior lights went on around the backyard, circling the pool.
Richardo's deep shadow hiding place was exposed. He had to act; flattening himself on the wall next to the patio doors. He went for the MP-443. The silencer caused the automatic

to get stuck in his pocket. Rich wrestled it for a moment. Then he realized he'd have to use his bare hands.

"Dimitri?" Roitman hissed, walking out.

(So, Richardo thought, the Tail had a name--Dimitri.)

Richardo ripped the automatic free of his pocket. He slipped behind and pushed the barrel of the automatic into the back of the German's head. "Hands on your head."

Roitman started. "Who?"

Richardo swung and clobbered Roitman with the side of the automatic. The German went down, out cold.

Roitman massaged his temples and regained consciousness. It took him a few moments to realize he had been tied to a patio chair by wire coat hangers. "Hey," he looked up at Richardo, "What's this all about?"

"You know what it's about."

"No," Roitman struggled hard against the wire bonds. "*Fick dich*, I don't. I honestly don't."

"My money. Where's my money?"

"I don't have a *ficken* clue."

"You better get a *ficken* clue but quick."

"Is this what Boyko was yelling about?"

"Yup."

"A million bucks?" pled Roitman. "I don't have your million bucks."

"Nudelman said you did."

"He's nuts."

"He said you took the wrong case—the one with my money."

"I didn't take any case. I don't have a case like that."

"I want my money."

"I don't have your fuckin' money."

Richardo whipped the barrel of the automatic across Roitman's face. It ripped the flesh at his mouth. Blood bubbled out and ran down Roitman's chin and neck.

"...de la Guarda, or whatever your *verdammt* name is—I don't have the case. I don't have the money. If you ask me, Boyko pulled a fast one on you, so don't lay the blame on me."

"What'd you mean by that?"

"By what?" Roitman hacked up phlegm from his throat and spat out blood and a gob of something.

"Whatever my name is?"

The German tilted his head sideways, blinking at Richardo. "There's something wrong with you. First I met you in the office it's like 'who is this guy?' Something ain't solid."

"You don't like Latinos?"

"You're about as Latino as my German grandfather."

"I just want my money."

"You'll never get it back...not from Boyko."

"I already got what I wanted from Nudelman." Richardo ambled behind the bound man.

Roitman's eyes followed the automatic leveled at his head.

"I don't have your money."

"I know you don't. You never did. What I want is for you to suffer like she did."

"What? Suffer like who?"

"Like my wife."

A swift shift of expression washed over Roitman's face. "That's it." He growled and jumped in the chair, straining to get loose from the wire ties. "Now I know who you are. It nagged at me. It nagged at me all day."

"And you will be the last. I got your two boyfriends in India. I put a bullet in Suka's head. But the cagey general cheated me and took his own life before I could pull the trigger. Nudelman is dead on the floor of his office. Now there's only you."

"I got muscle coming," Roitman gasped, threatened. "He'll take care of you."

"Like I took care of him?"

"Huh?"

"He's at the bottom of the pool."

"Wait...I can get you million bucks, just give me some time. You spare me for a million dollars?"

"You think money can save you?" Richardo pushed the automatic into the base of Roitman's neck. "Not for a million million dollars. Get my wife back."

The German squirmed and panted, the only sounds in the darkness.

"You son of a bitch."

"Curse me all you want. It's not going to change your fate."

Richardo clicked off the safety, pulled and let the receiver of the MP-443 slide back.

Roitman tensed.

Richardo knew if he was going to make a move it would be now.

Too late.

"*Pfffft...*"

Richardo put a single bullet into the base of Roitman's skull. Brains, blood, bone spewed out the man's forehead. He slowly pitched forward in the patio chair.

He cut the wire bonds and dragged the body by the collar to the edge of the pool. Billfold to cell phone, Richardo emptied the dead man's pockets. With his foot, Richardo pushed him over into the pool. "Piece of shit." He landed in a heap, a tangle of arms and legs next to Tail. Blood from their wounds pooled about their limbs and narrow worms leaked from the bodies snaking to the dirty water at the deep end of the pool.

Richardo rushed across the yard and into the house. His gloves were soft and wet with blood but would not leave fingerprints. He dashed from room to room, turning off lights and locking the front door. He slipped out the patio doors, closing them behind. In a moment, he got around the pool and to the stucco fence. Richardo was up and over into the neighbor's dark yard in almost one motion.

Growling noises from the shadows got his attention. Not waiting to identify nor attempt to calm the animal, Richardo crossed the yard at a dead run with the dog barking at his heels.

He got out of the yard and down the drive into his SUV while lights from houses started to flash on behind him.

Curious people alerted by the dog were coming out of their houses. Richardo saw them in his rearview mirror as he drove down the block. Turning a corner tight, with screaming tires, they were gone. He followed the green signs to the freeway entrance.

Already checked out at the Hilton, Richardo sped up, climbing the freeway on-ramp and merging into the late-night flow of headlights and shadowy cars.

GPS redirected him to the route out of San Diego and clear of California toward the Nevada border and Las Vegas.

He got on I-15 North and pushed past the speed limit. A deep breath and he calmed down. He'd been going on and on mindlessly, just on his training. Now he had time to think back at what he had done.

Sorting through the actions of the day, Richardo alarmed himself, partly due to him having survived virtually unharmed.

"Oh my God," he murmured. Setting the cruise control for 80 miles per, sighing, Richardo drove on through the blackness of night chasing his headlights on the asphalt. The room at Emigrant Isles waited.

He dwelled on what he had done but did not regret it. Not for those people.

Just after Beacon Station, a dusty road turned off into the desert night. Richardo drove the rutted road over a rise and out of sight of the interstate. He got out and broke down the automatic. He flung the trigger assembly deep into the starry desert darkness. The barrel went into the blackness in another direction. The handful of rounds he hurled wildly about. He dug a small hole with a trench shovel and changed into jeans and a polo shirt, burying Richardo's maroon suit, bolo tie, gloves, the lethal hypo and fedora. Taking out the sim cards from the cell phones and pocketing them, dropping the cell phone bodies onto the clothing—Richardo set the pile on fire and watched it burn.

Reaching Las Vegas around three in the morning, his flight to Phoenix was scheduled for eleven forty-five.

The casino bustled with activity and seemed crowded as Richardo crossed the lobby to the elevator. He could've sworn the skinny old lady at the slot machine had not left her chair in two full days. Her necklace of paper tickets had grown.

He switched on the light. The room was stuffy, but the bed was made with fresh towels hung in the bathroom. Tossing the satchel and attaché case on the bed, Richardo stripped down for a shower.

The hot water revitalized him. With the towel wrapped around his waist, Richardo rummaged through the briefcase. There were rubber band bound stacks of money that he fanned through and estimated to be over four hundred thousand dollars. A number of the folders had Russian names and papers inside.

"Bertoloni or Mr. Ogg would find these interesting," Richardo muttered.

There were a couple of thumb drives and some excel spreadsheets, but little else. He put the files and thumb drives into a bag and used the attaché case for the money and "his" booty. Nudelman's wallet had nearly a thousand dollars in U. S. currency, and not much else Richardo could use. A driver's license and some credit cards were all he thought useful to him. The Tail, Dimitri, had Ukrainian documents that Richardo thought might be of value to him if he went back to Ukraine. He did not resemble the former boxer though he might've passed with his driver's license photo showing a marked loss of fighting weight. And the dark-haired man's passport might be altered, making it useful for the elusive Richardo de la Guarda.

Dimitri, being the Tail, the muscle, the bottom rung of the ladder, had less than a hundred dollars to his name. Although, he had an international driver's license, single bank debit card and currency in mixed U.S. and Ukrainian bills.

Roitman's billfold, on the other hand, bulged with over five hundred dollars in small denominations, a U.S. driver's license, credit cards from Russian and U.S. banks and business cards. Richardo took the money. He'd keep the business cards for contacts and research in articles on Russian criminal activity in Southern California.

He stuffed the plastic bag into his satchel, locked the attaché case, set the digital bedside clock for ten in the morning and lay back into a mound of pillows watching the news.

CHAPTER 14

Rich headed back to a mess—the likelihood of extradition from the United States to India. Two United States Marshals sat drinking soft drinks (maybe he should tell Daisy to spike the soda pop) in The Ordinary waiting to take custody of him and hand him over to Indian authorities investigating the murder of Ukrainian criminal Irina "Suka" Franco and four others. (They apparently had not yet located Rich's fifth victim partially buried in the woods across the road from the villa.)

Part of him wanted to go back. Face the extradition and get the matter resolved. While another part urged a left turn and to run for his life. He doubted he could get a square deal from India, Russia or even the United States.

Rich might change direction to along the parallel, left and drive west of the prime, then right himself and head up the meridian, north of the equator to Eastern Oregon. In the shadow of the Three Sisters, no one knew him, no one would ever find him; moreover, no one cared and would not rat him out.

Borodavka was right. He had not gone through, nor completely grieved over the murder of Gisele. That leaden weight seemed to hang in the back of his mind constantly.

Taking an alternate route out of Phoenix, Rich went up through Colorado on I-40; then I-25 North to I-76. Driving into snow cells and over icy roads, he saw cars abandoned in the median covered in new snow and ice, showing signs of being there for more than one storm.

After the long, boring drive through northeast Colorado on I-76, where gas stations and a snack stop just did not exist, Rich merged onto I-80 between Sidney and Ogallala, Nebraska.

Weary, paranoia set in. He could see and almost read the headlines in the San Diego newspapers.

Russian Trio Found Murdered in Oceanside Beach.

A pair of foreign nationals were found murdered in an empty swimming pool in the toney Ocean Side Beach. The two were registered Ukrainians with work visas and employed by Nudelman Real Estate, San Diego.

The first victim, Dimitri Kosenko had a broken neck, while the second, Symon Roitman, a well-known real estate agent, was killed with a single bullet to the back of the head. The wound seemed to indicate he'd been executed.

Both men had extensive criminal records in their home countries but clean sheets in the United States.

A third victim, real estate broker Boyko Nudelman, was discovered in his office. He appeared to have suffered a massive heart attack, although foul play has not been ruled out.

A Panamanian businessman, last seen in the real estate office, is being sought for questioning.

The mobile phone buzzed twice. Rich heard Daisy pick up.

"The Ordinary bar."

"Daisy, it's...."

She cut him off immediately. "Boss...this is really a bad time to call." Her voice was muted as if she was talking through her hand muffling the phone.

"What're you talking about? It's my bar."

"They're here."

Rich did not need to ask who.

"They show up at any hour, every day," she went on. "I look up and they're at the table in the corner. I make small talk and they keep it even smaller while not really saying anything." She paused. "Except..." She lowered her voice to sound mannish. "We're here to see Mr. Rice. When will he be in?"

"And you say?"

"Don't know."

"Maybe I can sneak upstairs,"

"Don't try it. I wouldn't be surprised if they had The Ordinary staked out from a car out back."

His gut tightened. Rich sighed. They were silent.

"Go to your lawyer's."

"That or I'll get a room downtown. And the minute they leave, either call or text me."

"Okay." Daisy's voice sounded jittery.

They ended the call.

Rich pounded his open hand on the steering wheel.

Borodavka's house was in an older, less expensive tract of Omaha—not all that old, more from the late forties and fifties than the early twentieth century. Close to midnight, Rich drove past the small brick two-story house between Saddlecreek and Midtown. Each house in the area was situated on a small rise buttressed by retaining walls and separated by steep cement driveways. Every man, in his own way, had his nine hundred square foot castle on the hill. Rich drove down the block parking in a dark patch under a burnt-out streetlight.

Carrying his satchel, Rich walked down the street checking parked cars for occupants.

Spots of snow on the lawn of Borodavka's house revealed last Fall's leaves unraked. The lights were on. The curtains drawn. Rich stepped to the door.

He knocked.

"Who is it?" a gruff voice wanted to know. The gruff voice was a woman's, surprising Rich.

"Richard Rice," he called back. Then explained, "I'm a client of Mr. Borodavka."

Locks clattered on the other side of the door. Opened a crack, a short woman peered upward.

"He's still up."

"Let him in," Borodavka bellowed.

"Shut it, you'll wake the kids," the woman snapped back. She wore a robe of shiny material of such age the color was no longer distinguishable.

Rich slipped in. "Thank you."

The living room was small, overly warm and littered with children's toys, a playpen, books and newspapers. An oversized flat-screen television dominated one wall. A heavily made-up late-night chat show host talked to some giddy starlet. The furniture, couch and easy chairs, was old and assorted.

The whole house smelled of boiled cabbage and boiled beef.

"He's in the kitchen," she pointed.

"Okay." Rich crunched a plastic block as he crossed the living room.

On one side of the narrow kitchen were counters, appliances and a double ceramic sink. Borodavka sat at a round table on the other side, reading a graphic novel. He nursed a beer to wash down a cookie from a plateful. He glanced over.

"Richard, what brings you out this late?" He motioned to an empty seat next to a baby's highchair.

Exhaling, Rich wearily sat.

"I need a favor. I can't go to The Ordinary. The U.S. Marshals are there, waiting for me."

"They paid me a courtesy call too." The large lawyer wore a threadbare striped terrycloth robe over pajamas. He brushed cookie crumbs from his wild beard.

"Oh yeah?"

"They are VERY keen to get their paws on you."

The two looked at each other quietly.

"Made me think," the lawyer broke the silence. "It's more than India."

"I gather."

"What'd you plan to do?"

"Don't know," Rich admitted. "I was wondering if I could crash on your couch...just for tonight."

"Sure," Borodavka held back. "Well, I'll have to ask my wife. I'm sure she'll say yes."

"Thanks."

"What're you going to do after that?"

"Don't know."

"As your lawyer, I advise you to give yourself up."

"Not ready for that."

"Who would be? Though, it's the smart play, Richard."

"Why would you call that smart?"

"Cookie?"

"No, thanks."

With his mouth full and crumbs sputtering out, Borodavka explained. "Shows you believe you are innocent of any charges, a good citizen. You are throwing yourself on the mercy of the judge and shouldn't be extradited."

"No, I am not inclined to do that."

"I understand your reluctance."

Mrs. Borodavka turned off the television and left the living room, saying, "Lock up when you're ready to come to bed."

"Wait." Borodavka rose and spoke to his wife in the hallway. Rich caught some words among the hurried whispers.

"How long?"

"We're going to your mother's tomorrow."

The lawyer came back into the kitchen.

"She's okay with you staying the night."

"Not after that, though."

Borodavka shrugged. "Happy wife, happy life."

"Not saying I would—but what if I did turn myself in, what can I expect to happen?"

Borodavka sat and pondered. His eyes went upward; he munched the last cookie and toyed with his beard, considering.

"I don't actually know. Most of my practice is immigration and deportation to Central and South America. I have no clue what a criminal extradition to Europe is all about. I've never dealt with the Feds, Interpol or foreign governments." The lawyer leveled his gaze.

"I assume you'll be handed a summons to appear for an extradition hearing in federal court...but after that, I don't have a clue. A rag'n'bone immigration lawyer like me may not even be allowed in the hearing."

Rich hunched forward his head in his hands. "So my options are to surrender or go on the lam?"

"What would happen to The Ordinary?"

"I'd get a property manager to run the business."

"Do you really want to become a fugitive for the rest of your life?"

"Not sure."

"Not sure? Again, as your lawyer, I strongly advise you to give yourself up."

"That doesn't work for me."

"This India stuff will not go away."

"I could become Richardo de la Guarda for the rest of my life."

"You're not listening to me." An angry edge sliced through his lawyer's voice. "It's not just India that wants you—you understand that?"

"Panama is a nice place to live."

Borodavka drained the last of his beer and stood. "If you're going to ignore me, I'm going to bed. I get ignored there all the time." He wobbled unsteadily to the sink with the cookie plate and glass. "Bathroom's down the hall. There's a blanket on the couch."

While his lawyer talked, Rich went into the satchel and piled some stacks of the cash he'd conned out of Nudelman. He leafed through five stacks and lay the greenbacks on the table.

"I need you to hold this money for me and set up an account you can access to send me money."

"How much is that?"

"About two hundred thousand," Rich said. "You can take your retainer off that."

Borodavka whistled low and took the stacks. "I'll tuck it under the mattress and set up the account tomorrow." He slapped the stacks in the palm of his other hand and went to the hallway then stopped. "We can talk tomorrow. We both might make better sense after a good night's sleep."

"Thanks," Rich said.

"Turn out the kitchen light."

Rich arranged the rumpled odd-sized and colored pillows on the couch. He unlaced his boots and turned off the side table lamp. The room was dark but for a square of white light on the far wall, cast from the streetlight outside.

He covered himself with the woolen southwestern design blanket and lay back his head on his forearm. He stared at the ceiling.

CHAPTER 15

Rich sat flanked by a pair of U.S. Marshals in the International Lounge at O'Hare Airport.

Multi-racial and ethnic families with children mingled amongst couples and businessmen, some in native dress. A counter in a corner with uniformed airline representatives worked on reducing the queue stretching out from where they sat. The glass wall opposite had a wide vista looking out on the busy tarmac. Parked airliners from a variety of world carriers docked to gateways into the terminal. A vague smell of diesel fuel could be detected in the lounge.

"How long is this flight?" There was a hint of incredulity in the older, doughy black man sitting to Rich's right.

"For the tenth time...it's about seventeen hours," Rich replied in a monotone, his eyes set straight ahead.

"That's a long time to be in the air," the young, muscular Deputy U.S. Marshal, leafing through an inflight magazine on Rich's left, said.

"Yup."

"Is a plane able to fly that long?"

"Yeah," the older marshal chimed in. "Especially this plane."

"We'll find out. At least I won't have turnaround and have to come back the next day." Rich gave each marshal a smirk.

People eyed Rich as they passed through the lounge. They seemed to understand. Rich glared back. The marshals were considerate and had removed the handcuffs from Rich's wrists.

"Around about hour ten you will be glad you booked business class. The seats are wider and there is legroom to stretch out."

A middle-aged woman in navy blue skirt, matching jacket over a frilly white blouse, approached. Her long black hair was tightly bound in the back. Light make-up enhanced her tan complexion. She bent forward, hands clasped and spoke guardedly to the older marshal.

"We will be boarding in fifteen minutes." She gave Rich a quick wary glance. "You and your um, prisoner may board first."

"Sounds good."

"If you would follow me, we will go to the gate."

The young marshal, with a sigh, pitched the magazine onto a coffee table.

"Say bye-bye to the U.S.A, Mr. Rice."

"Not funny, deputy," the black marshal said.

Rich had no comeback to the deputy's comment. He gathered up a plastic bag with a couple of books and writing journal and walked between the marshals, each with a firm grip on Rich's arm above the elbow.

The orange numerals on the clock on Borodavka's mantle read 4:10. It was still dark outside. Rich had slept on and off, an hour here, half an hour there. From down the hall, he could hear noisy and deep snoring. Quickly Rich got out from under the blanket and swung his feet from the couch to floor. He laced up his boots and stood.

He let himself quietly out of the house. A biting chill greeted him outside. Hurrying up the block, he got in his truck. The seat was cold, the interior colder and the truck seemed reluctant to turn over. But it did.

Traffic was light to nonexistent. The traffic signal lights flashed orange, letting Rich speed through. In good time Rich reached The Ordinary. He went around the block checking the parked cars. Nothing seemed peculiar. With his remote, he drew back the gate to the gravel lot in back. Inside, he turned in his seat and watched the gate close.

Gathering his satchel and coat, Rich was out of his truck and to the stairs in a hurry.

Out of the corner of his eye, he caught movement in the shadows.

A cat?

Up the stairs two at a time, Rich unlocked the door with his key. He was inside and punching the entry code on the CCTV surveillance system.

Leaving the lights off, he made his way to the living room. Enough stray light from outside illuminated the gun safe black combination dial. He put in his conceal carry, passport and driver's license and anything else linking him to Richardo de la Guarda, the files and thumb drives (and SIM cards from the phones) from Nudelman's office; as well as the more than two hundred thousand dollars left over from the haul he'd grifted off the broker.

Shutting the heavy door and spinning the dial, there was a banging on the back door.

"U.S. Marshals, Mr. Rice. Open the door."

"Shit."

Taking a quick scurry around the flat, snapping lights on, Rich made sure nothing incriminating had been left laying out.

The knocking became harder, louder.

"Come on, Rice. We know you're in there. Open the door."

"Yeah...yeah. Be right there."

He swiped back the lock and opened the door. A pair of blue jacketed, obviously cold, United States Marshals stood on the landing. The older, a large black man, showed his five-pointed marshal's star; the other, younger and visibly shivering, held his identification up.

"I'm U. S. Marshal Hopkins," the black marshal said, giving his partner a head nod. "This is Deputy Marshal Edwards."

Rich held the door open but blocked it with his leg. "Very late, fellows. If you're not delivering a pizza, get off my landing."

"I wouldn't call this a friendly call. Are you Richard Vere Rice?"

Rich just stared back.

"Come on, man," Edwards said. "It's cold out here. Are you?"

Hopkins gave Edwards a disapproving look. "I apologize for my deputy. Are you Richard Rice?"

"You know I am. What's your business?"

The marshal reached into the inside pocket of his jacket.

Rich took a step back.

"Relax. We have a summons for you to appear at an extradition hearing in U.S. District Court." He held up a thick envelope.

"Give it to me...and go."

"Not as easy as that, I'm afraid."

A cold wind blew in through the door. Rich shook. "This is ridiculous. Get your asses in here."

The two shuffled in.

"Thanks."

"Man," Edwards said. "I thought I was going to freeze my ass off."

Rich closed the door.

"Okay. What the fuck is this all about? You just serving a summons for me to appear or what?"

"More complicated than that." Hopkins put the summons on the counter.

"You mind if I use your toilet?" Edwards asked.

Rich gave him a squint. "Yeah, if you don't get cute and snoop around. You don't have a search warrant."

"You invited us in."

"And I can kick your ass out too."

Hopkins, hands on the counter, dropped his head and shook it. He appeared tired, cold and fed up with his deputy.

"Edwards," he said. "Just use the damn toilet and come back."

"First door on the left."

The deputy hurried to the toilet.

"Sorry, Rice," Hopkins said. "Training."

"I get it. Pull up a stool. You want coffee or anything?"

"I'm good."

Rich picked up the envelope, slipped out the tri-folded papers. He scanned the first page. "Says the hearing is scheduled for two days from today."

"That is evidentiary and whether you qualify for bail. But they do turn them around pretty quickly."

Rich read on: "...extradition request for subject to be transported and surrendered to law enforcement authorities of the Republic of India."

The toilet flushed. Edwards came in buckling his belt.

"Thanks," he said. "Thought I would drown. What's in that big safe?"

"None of your damn business."

"We have to take you into custody." Hopkins said this quietly.

"What the fuck? I'm not going anywhere."

"Not how it works. And...you are considered a flight risk."

Rich stared at the two. He took a deep breath, trying to keep his compromise, but not doing a particularly good job of it.

"This is bullshit. Where are you taking me?"

"Tecumseh—if they have a spot. Or downtown."

Head down, Rich mulled over the situation. "It's damn early. I could use a couple hours of sleep."

"Me too."

"You can sleep on the drive," Edwards said, bringing out a pair of handcuffs from the back of his belt.

Hopkins put his hand out. "I don't think we will need those. Not yet."

Rich made no reply.

"Let me call this in." Hopkins unclipped a cell phone from his belt and turned aside, making a call.

Edwards rested the heel of his right hand on the butt of his 9mm service automatic holstered on his hip.

"No answer from Tecumseh." Hopkins said. "I'll try downtown."

"Can I close up my flat?"

Hopkins, phone to his ear, said. "I suppose. Edwards, keep an eye on him."

Rich changed into a sweatshirt and jeans and went through the flat, turning off lights. He paused at the bathroom door.

"You want to watch me piss?"

Edwards rolled his eyes upward.

"Well," Hopkins said as Rich came out of the bathroom. "I can't rouse anybody. We're headed downtown."

Hopkins in front, Edwards bringing up the rear, the marshals led a handcuffed Rich down the iron stairs. They walked him up the cold, pre-dawn street to an unmarked gray van. Edwards unlocked the side door. Hopkins covered Rich's head as they helped him up the step and into the van.

Rich, stooped over, sat on a metal bench that ran along the side of the van. A metal mesh divided the driver and passenger seats from the back of the van.

"Turn on the heat," Edwards said, buckling the seat belt on the passenger seat.

"Aren't you supposed to read me my Miranda rights?"

"You're not under arrest," Hopkins said, looking left and right and pulling out of his parking spot.

"Sure feels like it."

"We're taking you into custody...but you're not being arrested."

Edwards laughed.

"It's bullshit."

"Yeah...it is," Hopkins slowly agreed. "But it is what it is." He glanced right and turned left.

"We just do what they tell us to do."

"Which is mostly pick 'em up and drop 'em off."

Rich braced himself to stay seated in the bumping and bouncing back of the van.

They pulled into the underground garage at 111 South 18th Plaza.

"Been here before," Rich grumbled.

Hopkins got out, while Edwards went and opened the van's side door.

"Hold on," Edwards said, his hand up.

The older marshal tried the door handle (locked) and banged on the metal door.

No answer.

Rich slouched on the bench, waiting, watching, mentally debating whether to run or sit tight.

Hopkins hammered on the metal door, and muttered, "Answer the damn door."

Eventually, a yawning face appeared on the other side of the glass and wire window in the door. The man had more tattoos than most prisoners.

"What the hell are you guys doing here?"

"Hoodie in custody."

"It's not even five in the morning."

"No shit," Edwards said, assisting Rich down from the van.

They escorted Rich into the processing area. Hopkins handed over a manila folder with Rich's papers.

"Empty your pockets."

Rich twisted his shoulder forward, showing his handcuffed wrists.

Edwards turned out Rich's pockets and spilled everything onto the counter. Items were cataloged and bagged. Rich had to contort himself to make a signature.

"What size you wear?"

"XL."

"You got a cell for him?"

"No. I have a holding cell."

"Don't just throw him into population." Hopkins sounded irritated. "He's not one of the bad guys."

"When's his hearing?"

"Day after tomorrow."

"I'll have a cell for him later today. Right now, all I got is a holding cell and an empty office."

"Put him in the empty office," Edwards insisted.

"Take him into that side room." Then he said to Rich. "Strip down to your civvies. Once I check to see if you're smuggling a machine gun up your butt, you can put on your jailhouse orange tuxedo."

Edwards took off the cuffs from Rich's wrists and pushed him into the office. The jailer, behind the young marshal, threw in a coarse woolen blanket and small pillow. He frisked Rich from hair to left then right foot.

"Drop your civvies and spread your cheeks." The jailer pulled on a latex glove.

The office door locked, leaving Rich alone in the empty office. He found the black-tinted plastic dome concealing the camera in a corner. That didn't stop him from checking the locked door and latched windows. The windows were more glass laminate wire mesh. There was no way out.

"Wake up," a jailer loudly said, walking into the office. "Your lawyer's here to see you."

Rich sat up from the bench and rubbed the sleep crust from his eyes.

Two brown uniformed jailers led Rich down a walled cement corridor. He got dirty looks from every cell he passed.

"Number eleven." One of the jailers pointed to a blurry plexiglass window at the far end of the roomful of cubicles. Borodavka's hairy face waited on the other side. Rich took the phone from a hook on the side.

"They treatin' you all right?"

"I guess."

"I came to bail you out," the lawyer said. "But they've moved up your hearing to this afternoon. No sense in bailing you out for a couple of hours. You just chill here for a while."

"Are you going to be at the hearing?"

"Yeah." Borodavka pulled out a pile of papers from his briefcase. "This is not like a grand jury hearing. I can be there and advise you. We can present evidence as explanatory. This serves to undermine the government's case for extradition. The evidence is weighed by the judge whether explanatory or contradictory. Contradictory evidence will be thrown out."

Rich stretched. "I'm still half-asleep. I'll follow your lead."

"I got a text from that odd man you told me about...your spook friend."

"Spook friend?"

"The little guy. The spook."

"Oh." Rich woke up. "Deputy Director Honesto Ogg. What's he want?"

"To be there. Says he wants to stand up for you."

Rich laughed derisively. "He's a bottle of beer shy of five foot. Can we get someone taller to stand up for me?"

Shouts and hip-hop beats, boasts and confrontation filled the cell block.

Rich lay on the bunk of a six by eight-foot cell. Conflicting emotions of anger and defeat waged war back and forth across his thoughts. It seemed futile, yet he vowed to fight his situation until all the exigencies were exhausted. Jail seemed the best place to let loose of his pent-up grief and come to grips with the murder of Gisele. The perpetrators had been dealt with in a way fit for killers. Those still standing on the field should take notice; he would not stop until revenge was his. And yet, she was gone—forever. A price nearly more than he could bear.

"What ya in for?" A black youth with sagging jeans, rolled t-shirt sleeves, and a hairnet on his hair extensions asked.

"Spitting on the sidewalk," was Rich's surly reply.

"Keep it to you-self then, chief."

"I just don't want to talk about it."

"That I can dig. You look like you got bread. You evah need sum'thin' sum'thin' let me know."

Jailers came down the row of cells, keys and equipment jingling. The youth stole a quick glance and ambled in the other direction.

"All right, Rice," one jailer said, using a big flat key to unlock the beat-up cell door. "Time for your hearing."

Rich shuffled out and was stopped for a pat-down. The youth watched at the top of the row of cells. He gave Rich a one-finger salute. Rich replied with a nod up.

The jailers clapped cuffs on Rich's wrists and led him toward the cellblock door.

They went from corridor to corridor, ending up in a holding cell behind the courtroom. They took off his cuffs.

Three Hispanics sat on a padded bench. One had a thick folder of papers in a school binder. The other two had notes and envelopes.

"I know you," a middle-aged Hispanic said to Rich. "I mean I seens you before someplace."

"I don't know where," Rich replied.

The wood laminate door on an opposite wall opened and an overweight bald man in a brown uniform, heavily armed, stepped in. Rich assumed he was the bailiff.

"Gonzalez, you're up," he almost shouted.

The middle-aged man arranged his binder and papers as he stood and crossed the holding cell. He stopped at the door, half-turning, looking at Rich.

"Jorge," he said. "Jorge works for you."

Rich dropped his head.

He disappeared into the courtroom.

"Deportation?" one of the others asked Rich.

"Where they going to deport him—Plymouth Rock?"

They laughed. Rich pretended to join in.

None of the three returned to the holding cell. Rich, last in line, waited for the bailiff to call him.

"Rice. Let's go."

A usual looking courtroom, with judge's bench, court reporter, two tables (one manned by a well-dressed legal team, the second empty) and a scattered group of spectators in the gallery. Rich spotted Borodavka wearing a mustard-colored suit jacket and matching slacks in the front row. Honesto Ogg, in dark suit, moved forward and seated himself next to the large lawyer.

The bailiff handed the woman judge a folder. She had big, brushed-back grey-blonde hair, overly rouged cheeks and gaudy earrings.

"This isn't another deportation?" she asked, taking the folder.

"No. This is the international extradition," the bailiff replied, motioning Rich to go to the empty table.

"Oh," she said. "Give me a minute to look over the notes and documents." Then to the recorder, she said, "Rice v. United States" and added the case number.

After a short interval, the judge closed the folder.

"Mr. Rice, if you would stand, please." The judge waited as Rich struggled to his feet. "This is an extradition hearing, the start of a process. It's not a criminal trial, nor a deportation hearing. I want you to understand this from the get-go." She leaned forward, directing her comments to the recorder.

"The court recognizes Mr. Rice is represented by legal counsel, Douglas Borodavka. How're you, Doug?"

"Fine, yer honor," he responded. "Good to see you, Consuelo."

"And you, Sir?" She asked Ogg.

"Honesto Ogg."

"Are you a lawyer?"

"No, I..."

"Please return to the gallery then."

Ogg sheepishly retreated to his seat in the front row.

"And the United States is represented by..?"

"U.S. District Attorney Miles Whittaker," the man at the other table said. "And Assistant U.S. District Attorney April Chandler. The other two members of the team are interns from the office, yer honor."

"Fine. I have one rule in this courtroom. Miles, you know it, and I am sure Doug knows it well. This is MY courtroom." She let that sink in.

The judge changed gears. "Mr. Rice, this is, as I previously stated, an extradition hearing and I don't imagine you have ever been in such a hearing before."

"No, yer honor."

"That was sort of rhetorical. You didn't need to answer."

"Sorry."

"And I didn't need that either. I understand you're anxious...calm down." The judge smiled.

"Firstly, the court needs you to state your full name."

"Richard Vere Rice."

"Your address?"

Rich gave the address of The Ordinary.

"Your occupation?"

"I own a bar in South Omaha."

"Named?"

"The Ordinary."

"Unusual name. Do you swear to tell the truth and nothing but the truth?"

"Yes, yer honor."

"Now you can be seated."

"Okay...here's what the hearing is all about. I am going to see if we can tick these off while I list them.

"An extradition hearing is not a criminal trial and not held to ascertain guilt. The intention of the court is to find evidence establishing probable cause that the fugitive committed the offense or offenses underlying the request for extradition."

The judge paused, then went on.

"The extradition hearing addresses the existence of a valid extradition treaty." The judge looked from the folder. "Mr. Whittaker, this extradition request comes from..."

The U.S. District Attorney stood with a pad. "The extradition request was delivered to the United States State Department from the Republic of India. The United States and India have had a longstanding extradition treaty."

"Okay. This hearing is to establish the identity of the extraditee," the judge said. "And we have done that. Richard Rice is on the request to the State Department and Criminal Division Office of International Affairs."

"And if I may, yer honor," Whittaker chipped in. "The crime for extradition, murder, is covered by the existing treaty."

"The court needs to verify whether the documentation is complete and authenticated." The judge shuffled through the folder. "That is something I want to come back to later.

"This hearing will establish whether probable cause exists that the extraditee committed the offense in question. And the court will meet other requirements under the extradition treaty." The judge closed the folder. "The government will present documentary evidence these issues have been met. The government also has the burden of establishing probable cause. Mr. Borodavka, Mr. Rice, do you understand the proceedings so far?"

"Yes, yer honor," Rich's lawyer replied.

Rich sat silent and glowering, powerless in this arena.

"This hearing will be more lenient with evidence and not bound by Federal Rules of Evidence. Depositions, warrants and other papers may be used as evidence," the judge said. "Incidentally, hearsay is permitted."

"Yer honor," Borodavka stood. "I understand the extraditee may present evidence as 'explanatory' and serves to contest the government's showing of probable cause."

"Correct. But the evidence is limited and can be only 'explanatory' and not contradictory."

"Gotcha."

The judge chuckled at Borodavka's response.

"I noticed in the jacket there is an Interpol Red Notice. That and the documentation is something I want to come back to later. Mr. Whittaker, I need to hear the extradition request from India."

"Certainly, yer honor," the government lawyer said. "If you don't mind, I will have Ms. Chandler read the request."

"Certainly." The judge laced her fingers under her chin and braced her elbows on the bench top. "Tell me a story, Ms. Chandler."

Borodavka, speaking rapidly as he wrestled his large self from behind the table, out of the chair and to his feet. "Yer honor, before Ms. Chandler lulls the courtroom to sleep with a fairy tale the government has concocted, I would like the court to be aware the extraditee does not have the same documents as the court and government.'

"How do you explain that, Mr. Whittaker?"

Whittaker, also standing, put his hands out. "Interns, yer honor."

"Clunk, Mr. Whittaker." The judge was not amused. "That ain't gonna fly in my court." She passed her folder to the bailiff. "While Ms. Chandler spins her yarn, the bailiff will copy all information and documents I have been provided and make sure Misters Borodavka and Rice have the same."

The bailiff, with the judge's folder, disappeared through a side door.

"Ms. Chandler, you may proceed."

"Thank you." She was late twenties, thin as a wheat cracker blonde with a long severe face and no-nonsense voice. She wore a plain dark skirt and off-white blouse. The matching jacket hung off the back of her chair. "The Republic of India Criminal Division asserts that six weeks past Richard Rice traveled to Ranikhet, India and stayed at the West View Inn, Mall Road, for the sole purpose of committing murder.

"Mr. Rice is a citizen of the United States.

"He is sought as the perpetrator of five murders.

"Depositions and interrogations involve individuals who claim Mr. Rice selected the West View Inn for its close proximity to the Russian Federation-owned villa and that Mr. Rice disguised himself as an indigent person of Indian origin to deceive the occupants of the villa: Irina 'Suka' Franko and four other foreign nationals—mostly Ukrainian and Russian.

"To further disguise his deeds, Mr. Rice set fire to the villa. (The villa is property under the ownership of the Federation of Russia.)

"The Republic of India seeks to try Mr. Rice in India court on five counts of murder and two charges of arson and destruction of private property."

The courtroom was quiet.

"That's it?"

"I paraphrased, yer honor."

"And documents support these changes?" the judge asked. "The bailiff hasn't returned with our copies."

Depositions from the owner of West View Inn, Evie Somebody, where Mr. Rice stayed. Transcribed interrogations from a taxi driver named Gupta and an Indian Army Major Babbar, assigned to a regiment stationed at Kumaon. There are also many emails between various foreign embassies in India.

Rich scrawled on a yellow pad 'Eyewitnesses?' and slid it under Borodavka's eyes. He nodded.

"Any of these individuals claim to be eyewitnesses to the alleged criminal acts committed by my client?"

"I would venture not. Mr. Whittaker?"

He shrugged. "If not indicated, I would assume that as well."

"Yer honor?"

"Mr. Rice."

"May I comment on this?"

"I don't have any objection to that. Mr. Whittaker?"

Whittaker raised his hands as if to say *sure, why not.*

"I know a little about Indian courts. They want eyewitnesses, especially for a capital crime such as murder," Rich said.

"I will note that," the judge replied.

The bailiff returned with copies of the judge's folder.

Whittaker twiddled his pen between his fingers while the judge and Borodavka (with Rich leaning over to see) leafed through the folders.

"It appears no one interrogated was even remotely an eyewitness."

"So, this is all hearsay evidence?"

"Apparently."

"Mr. Rice, were you a guest at..." the judge scanned a sheet of paper. "...the West View Inn in Ranikhet, India?"

"Yes, I was."

"And that was in the time frame the criminal charge asserted?"

"It was."

"And did you disguise yourself in order to commit the crimes alleged?"

"I did not."

"It appears the Interpol Red Notice is the only thing pushing Mr. Rice's extradition. That's a question for you, Mr. Whittaker."

"Yes, yer honor."

"Flimsy," the judge said. "I need more explanation why the murder of these five people and the destruction of this villa has caused such an international commotion." She searched through the folder. "There are emails back and forth from State and the DOJ, and more than two foreign governments." Glancing up, the judge asked, "Mr. Boro-davka, can your client shed some light on this?"

Rich was reluctant to say anything. "I can, but I think this guy," he jerked his thumb over his shoulder, "Honesto Ogg, would be more helpful."

"Who? Him? Not the lawyer?"

"Yes."

"Let's hear what you have to say."

"Not in open court," Ogg said, pushing through the gate.

"Approach," the judge waggled her fingers. "Join us, Mr. Whittaker. Mr. Rice, you can stay at the table."

Ogg stood too short to look over the top of the judge's bench. She brought him around to the side.

Rich heard Ogg introduce himself "Assistant Deputy Director Southeast Asia Central Intelligence Agency, Special Ops." He verified it with identification. "I'm a dust man...picking up after people." The Judge's expression showed surprise. Surprise wasn't in Whittaker's face.

"The hell..." she muttered.

Ogg's voice lowered and he spoke to the judge and he spoke mostly to the judge. When they broke up Ogg smiled at Rich as he walked back to the gallery. He paused as he walked by.

"Interesting events in San Diego," he whispered.

"Don't know what you're talking about," Rich answered, staring straight ahead.

"Thank you, Director Ogg. Quite a compelling tale. This explains emails in the jacket from the DOJ, as well as the Russian Federation and the Republic of India. You are a popular fellow, Mr. Rice." The judge made notations in her folder then continued. "The complexion of this hearing has changed somewhat. We won't be able to resolve the extradition this afternoon. Mr. Borodavka, will you be asking for bail for your client?"

"Yes."

"Yer honor, the government opposes bail, considering Mr. Rice a flight risk."

"Noted, but the court recognizes Mr. Rice owns a local business, so I am inclined to disagree with Mr. Rice being a flight risk. Bail is set at one hundred thousand dollars. The next scheduled hearing on this matter is Wednesday at one o'clock." She paused. "Any questions? Comments?" Her eyes went from table to table. "Since there are no objections from either side, this hearing is adjourned."

For a long time, Rich did not move while the courtroom emptied. Ogg left before Rich could corral him and ask what he said to the judge. He knew what the mention of San Diego referenced.

But Borodavka said as he packed his briefcase, "Ogg says you two are even now."

The bailiff stood in the middle of the courtroom, hands clasped, waiting on Rich.

"Rich? Rich?" his lawyer touched Rich's shoulder. "Rich?"

Rich roused himself.

"I am going to post your bail while the bailiff takes you to processing. I will meet you there." The bearded lawyer asked Rich, "Are you okay?"

"Yes. I just don't have a good feeling about all this."

Borodavka closed the metal clasp of his leather case.

"I don't see this turning out as anything but bad," Rich added. "Too many," Rich murmured to no one.

"I'm sorry...what?"

"Too many people. Too many powerful people. Too many governments. They all want my hide."

"You're exaggerating," Borodavka said.

"No, I'm not. Not even close."

"Come on, let's get you out of orange and back into civilian clothes," the bailiff said trying to make a joke, leading Rich through the holding cell door.

Driving Rich back to The Ordinary, Borodavka asked, "Mind if I think out loud?"

"No problem—only keep your eyes on the road," Rich said, "and I can join in."

"Fine." The lawyer thought a moment, then said, "It seems India is the principal seeking your extradition, but it's a half-hearted attempt. I mean India's evidence is circumstantial and hearsay. You were in Delhi and that other town at the time of the events."

"Ranikhet," Rich corrected.

"Yeah. The innkeeper says you stayed at the place near the villa. She claims she saw you disguised as a beggar."

"Claims. She never saw me disguised nor spoke to me as the beggar."

"Uh-huh. And she says she treated a wound on your foot that was not dissimilar to a gunshot wound."

"Which I told her occurred while on a hike."

"And there's the Indian Army Major whose testimony reads more like a woman scorned than an army intelligence officer."

"I was rather abrupt with Major Babbar and said very little."

"In the written testimony, he rambles on about your typical American arrogance, prejudice and lack of respect for other nationalities."

Rich broke out laughing.

"That might be funny, but Interpol's Red Notice is not."

"The major struck me as a jumped-up tea boy." Any amusement left Rich. "I agree the Interpol involvement is serious."

"I didn't know why at first."

"I have a good idea why," Rich interrupted.

Borodavka stopped at a red light. He half-turned to Rich. "Let me finish. We may both have the same idea. It's not India behind this—it's the Russian Federation that wants you."

"Go on."

The light turned green and the car behind Borodavka honked. He drove on. "There's no extradition treaty between the U.S. and the Russians, but there is a treaty with Russia and India. They want to get you to India where they can snatch you and take you to their jurisdiction. Using Interpol and the Red Notice is a lure."

"My thinking as well. Do you know how long it takes a case to go to trial in India?"

"Haven't a clue."

"Ten years on average. I could be rotting in Yerwada Central Jail for ten years before I see the inside of an India courtroom."

"That won't happen," Borodavka said.

"Oh? Why are you so certain? The current administration seems way too buddy-buddy with the Russians."

"That may be true, but if the judge rules in favor of the government's case, I will slap a Writ of Habeas Corpus on them."

"Habeas Corpus?"

"It acts as an appeal in extradition cases," Borodavka explained. "Immediately if and after a certificate of extradition is verified, the extraditee may petition for Writ of Habeas Corpus—28 U.S.C. 92241. It is considered an appeal and the court may stay the court orders."

"You'll put in a motion to hear the entire case?"

"Murder, arson and all that in a U.S. Court."

"I don't think a U.S. court would hear it," Rich said.

"My turn to ask why."

"With all the hearsay and circumstantial evidence, a U.S. court would throw it out."

"Now you're thinking like a lawyer."

"God help me."

Borodavka pulled into a parking space on the street by The Ordinary.

"So even if the judge rules in favor of extradition in this round, we have options to take it into the next round."

"Okay." Rich gathered up his folder and other papers. "Good to know. In my head, I was already stuck in an India prison waiting years to go to trial."

"I understood that. I will see you in court Wednesday— or call if something important comes up prior to the hearing."

They shook hands.

"Thanks, Doug," Rich said climbing out of the car.

"Can you call an electric cart to take us to the gate?" Edwards, the young marshal asked the airline representative.

"Certainly," she said.

An African family gave the trio a wide berth as they waited for the electric cart by the lounge door.

"Did you shower this morning?"

"Ha. Ha," Hopkins, the older marshal said.

The airline agent approached. "The cart is waiting outside. You may want to hurry. People think it's free and are jumping on."

"Okay. Thanks."

"Hook'em?" the young marshal held up a shiny pair of handcuffs.

"We going to need'em, Rice?"

"Not for me."

They went out the lounge door to the crowded, noisy, bustling corridor to the terminal gates. Faceless people going to boarding and deplaning swarmed up and down.

"Git yo ass off mah car," the elderly black driver said, shooing away a millennial-aged couple. "Day tink'n eferthang fer dem."

"We're your riders."

"Hops on."

They put Rich second seat behind Hopkins up front next to the driver. Edwards settled in by Rich.

Beep. Beep, the driver slowly parted the heavy flow of people rolling carry-ons or herding their kids or just half running to their gate or baggage claim.

Rich scanned the corridor and wondered if there was a chance.

"Gates?"

The older marshal told the driver. They worked their way to the righthand side.

Beep. Beep, the passengers parted for the electric cart.

"Next time I travel, this is the way to get to my gate," Edwards smirked at Rich.

He gave the marshal no response, studying faces as they drove by. They were nearing the gate. Once on board, his fate was sealed.

A break in the crowd and the driver stepped on it. As he did a second cart appeared through the break in the crowd. It was coming right at them—extremely fast.

"Yo on da wrong side," the driver shouted.

Too late. The carts collided at full speed.

Rich's cart was thrown up on its side. He grabbed a railing and held on. Screams from passengers around them mixed with the sounds of the skidding cart. Rich saw Hopkins thrown from his seat and tumble into passengers, knocking them down like tenpins.

"Bernie," the young marshal cried out as the cart crashed in the glass exterior of a restaurant bar. Rich clung to the handrail and ducked as glass showered around them.

The cart came to a stop just inside the bar.

"You stay here, or I'll goddamn shoot you," Edwards screamed at Rich as he untangled from the cart and barstools and ran, brushing the glass off, slipping on glass shards, to the older marshal. Hopkins was down, his arms and legs twisted at odd angles, surrounded by injured passengers.

Rich pulled himself up and vaulted over the side of the cart, pushing his way through bar patrons crowding forward to view the accident.

"We'll need an ambulance," Rich shouted. "Where's your back entrance?"

The bartender pointed to an unmarked back door. "I'll call 9-1-1." He pressed a button under the bar. A buzzer sounded and a red light lit over the door. Rich stiff-armed the door open and was momentarily blinded by bright sunlight over the airport tarmac.

He scrambled and felt his way downstairs and jogged toward the main terminal. Baggage carts and tugs whizzed past. He kept to the shade under an overhang. Ducking low under jetways connected to airliners, Rich reached the terminal. A pair of baggage handlers came out a door, pocketing badges. Rich slipped behind them and caught the heavy door before it closed.

The large room was baggage collection and conveyor belts from the ceiling fed checked bags for each airline flying out of the gates off the corridor above.

Rich weaved his way through.

"Hey," a handler yelled over the noise of belts and baggage banging. "Where's you going?" The man was loading a cart trailer.

"On break," Rich shouted back.

The man waved and went back to his job.

Rich found the door out and stepped in a white-tiled hallway. He briskly walked by a time clock and breakroom and baggage handlers going up and down.

"Attention," came over the loudspeaker. "Security Alert. The International Terminal is on security alert and locked down." Airline departure delays due to the security alert started coming over the speakers.

A red exit sign showed over a door at the end of the hallway. Rich made for it.

The door burst wide and black-uniformed SWAT and helmeted, heavily armed airport security charged through.

Rich went to the wall to get out of the way.

"Tarmac?" A squad member yelled his question through a plexiglass shield at Rich.

"Down, then left." Rich pointed.

"Thanks. Put a man on the door." And they ran down the hallway.

"What happened?" Rich asked the SWAT at the door.

"Don't know yet. What're you doing?"

"Off my shift."

The SWAT waved him through.

Rich found himself in a vast, nearly full dirt parking lot. He walked up and down the aisle of cars looking for models built before 2000. These were usually not equipped with car alarms as a standard. He found one.

Rich vanished.

ALGONQUIN

When Royce Partridge learns his boyhood pal Toby Bergman is dying of cancer, he returns to the small town of Algonquin, Illinois on the Fox River where they grew up. Royce left Algonquin 40 years ago. Progress in the form of strip malls, subdivisions and congested traffic has changed the once bucolic river  town. Royce surprises Toby in the hospital and finds him slipping fast. Royce stays in Algonquin at a quaint Victorian bed & breakfast.

Despite the heavy hand of progress, Royce can see the small town he and Toby raced mopeds around as teenagers. But it is down on the banks of the Fox River that Royce re-lives the wild adventure he, Toby and two other friends had the summer of 1964 before they started high school.

Available from Amazon and Amazon Kindle, as well as www.cortbooks.com

SISTERS' SECRET

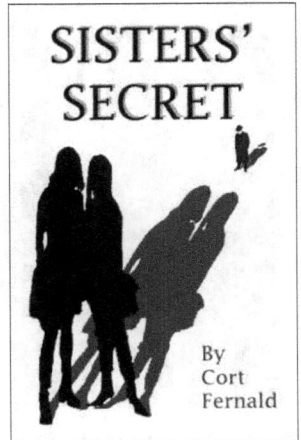

Sisters' Secret is a novel of grief and obsession. Mike Smith's beloved wife, Rebecca, is raped and murdered by unknown assailants. The police haven't a clue. Mike tries to lose himself in his work, to get on with his life. Months later, he attends his high school reunion. There he learns his high school girlfriend and her younger sister were abducted and gang raped. The crime was never reported.

Mike is horrified, but moreover, he believes he knows who among his classmates committed this crime.

Mike sets out to expose the criminals. But in so doing, he puts his life at risk

Available from Amazon and Amazon Kindle, as well as www.cortbooks.com

KEEPER of an ORDINARY

Rich pulled out the Glock and aimed into the black. Blam... Blam... Blam... light flashed and brass casings spit out the receiver.

Some problems can only be solved by a gun. Investigative reporter Rich Rice learns this when the Russian mafia comes after him for writing about their sex slave and human trafficking in Chicago. An assassin's bullet wounds Rich, forcing him to flee. Known as The Keeper, he hides out in South Omaha. Despite his best efforts to remain invisible, the Russians find him. Only then will the gun end it – dead or alive.

Available from Amazon and Amazon Kindle, as well as www.cortbooks.com

Reader Comments

"They say the first sentence makes a book. The first sentence grabbed me." R Jas

"Loved the book. I started and didn't put it down until I finished. I was surprised at the great ending!" R. Hendley

KEEPER TRIAL AND VENGEANCE

He traveled halfway around the world for revenge. Used as 'bait' by the FBI to lure the Russian Mafia out of hiding, investigative journalist and owner of The Ordinary bar in South Omaha, Rich Rice survives a savage gun battle. He survives only to be under subpoena by a grand jury. He faces indictment on multiple counts of murder. In Nebraska, that's an automatic ticket to the electric chair. Rich pleads self-defense and qualified immunity.

"I will leave you dead...without killing you." While on trial, Rich's wife Gisele is kidnapped by Russians under the thumb of Mafia madam Suka Franko. The Russian madam has fled to the subcontinent. Out for revenge, Rich travels to India in search of Suka Franko. The final showdown is not in India, but in Odessa, Ukraine, with Suka's father, ex-KGB General Ivan Franko.

Available from Amazon and Amazon Kindle, as well as www.cortbooks.com

WEST of ANTIPATHY

There's a joy in writing short stories, a wonderful sense of reward when you pull certain things off.   Tobias Wolff

The nine short stories that comprise this collection were written between 2014 and 2018. The stories were primarily writing exercises and mental challenges to keep my pen sharp and my wit sharper while researching and outlining novel projects.

Among these stories are thrillers, mysteries and suspense. A couple have a flick of humor and a wink of introspection. But each is an earnest attempt to tell a story in an entertaining way. If you are surprised, the story is a success. If you smile, the story has achieved its goal. If you are frightened, then there is something very real in the story.

Available from Amazon and Amazon Kindle, as well as www.cortbooks.com

ABOUT THE AUTHOR

Shortly after finishing *Keeper Coup de Grace*, Cort Fernald's fifth novel and the sequel to his thrillers *Keeper of an Ordinary* and *Keeper Trial & Vengeance*, Cort died of pancreatic cancer on April 3, 2020, after a yearlong battle.

Cort's other novels include *Algonquin*, a story of awakening set in the mid-sixties and *Sisters' Secret*, a thriller set in Park Forest, Illinois, the model of a post-World War II suburb. *Sisters' Secret* shows the dark side of the perfect, planned community.

Cort also wrote a collection of nine short stories in *West of Antipathy*.

Cort held a degree in English from Southern Oregon University and did graduate work in journalism at the University of Oregon.

Cort became a member of the Nebraska Writers Guild and was highly active in the literary scene, taking on the responsibility of Editor of the Nebraska Anthologies, *Voices of the Plains*, for the first and second editions.